SCURVY DOGS

AND THE

DINOSAUR BONEYARD

Kevin Frank

Kane Miller

A DIVISION OF EDC PUBLISHING

First American Edition 2019
Kane Miller, A Division of EDC Publishing

For information contact:
Kane Miller, A Division of EDC Publishing
P.O. Box 470663
Tulsa, OK 74147-0663
www.kanemiller.com
www.edcpub.com
www.usbornebooksandmore.com

Library of Congress Control Number: 2018942392

Manufactured by Regent Publishing Services, Hong Kong, China
Printed August 2020 in ShenZhen, Guangdong, China
3 4 5 6 7 8 9 10

ISBN: 978-1-61067-835-3

For C.G.F.
and for you

Chapter One

On a deserted island somewhere in an uncharted ocean, four Scurvy Dogs searched for buried treasure.

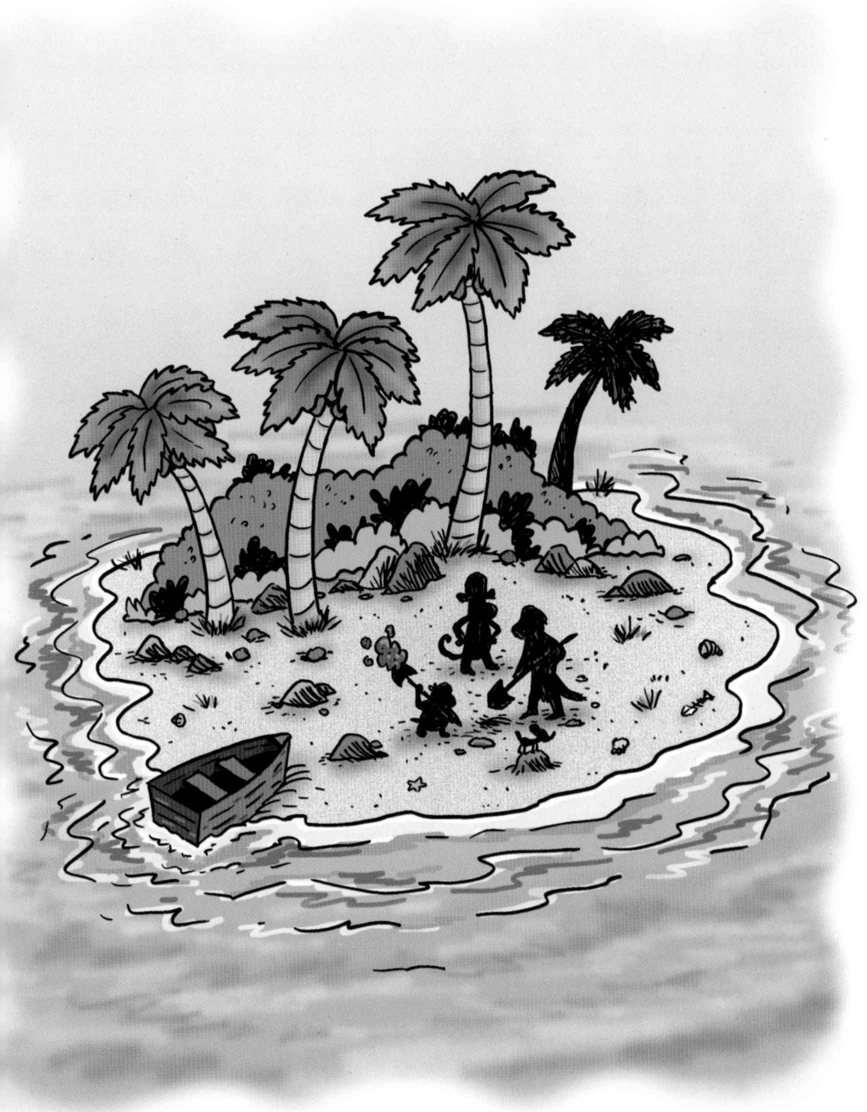

Captain Hooktail was in command, First Mate Chubbs and Helmsman Patch were digging, and Tinkles stood guard against cats.

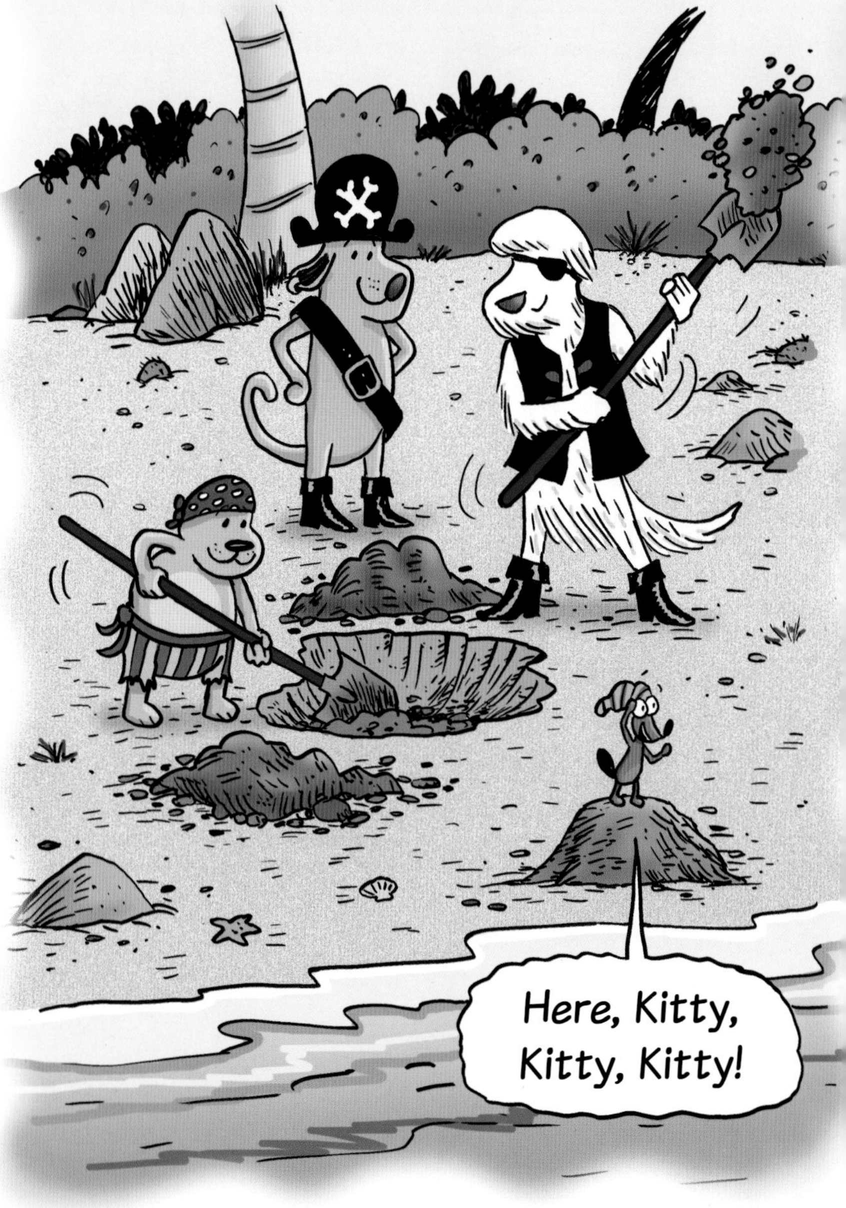
Here, Kitty, Kitty, Kitty!

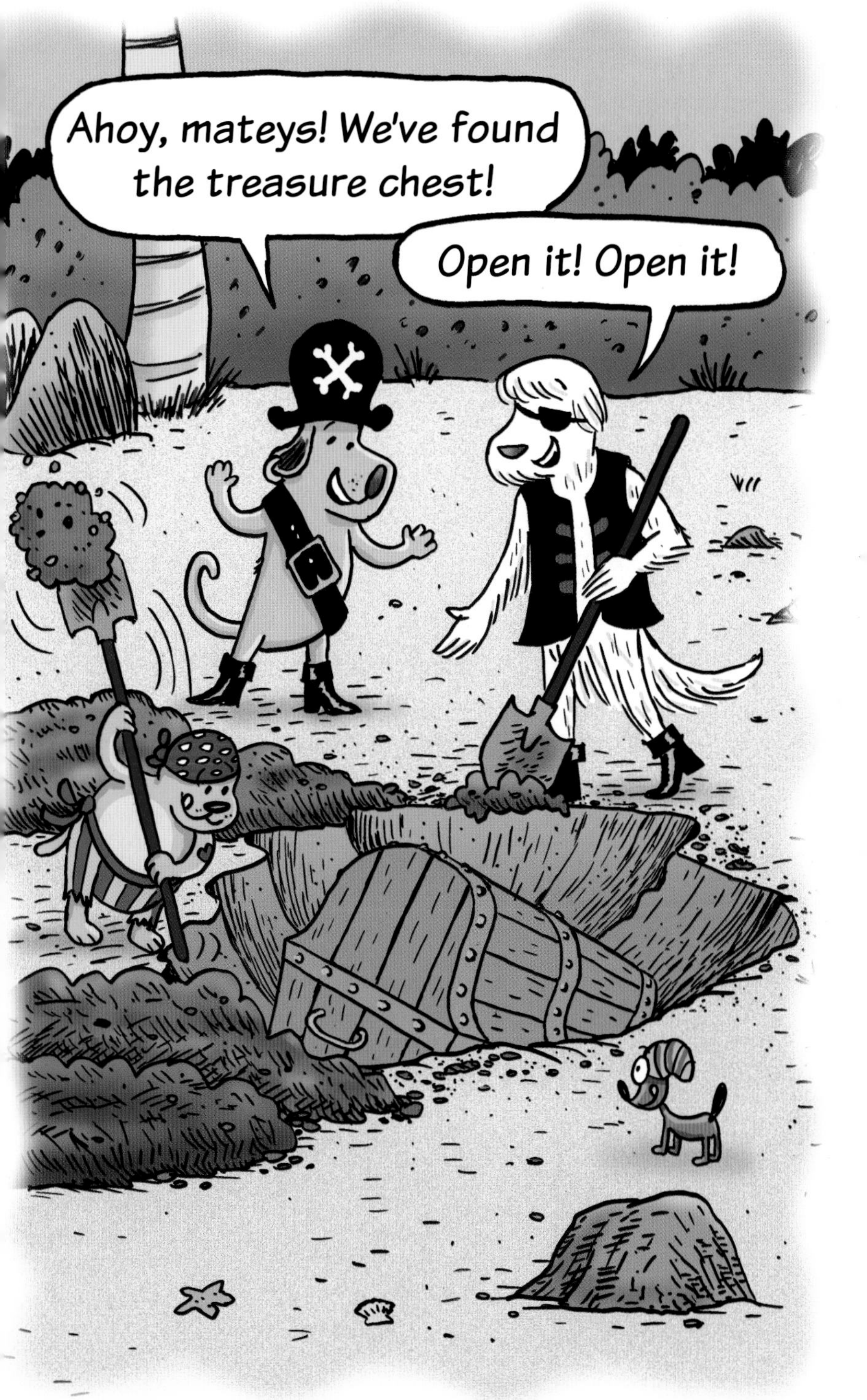
Ahoy, mateys! We've found the treasure chest!
Open it! Open it!

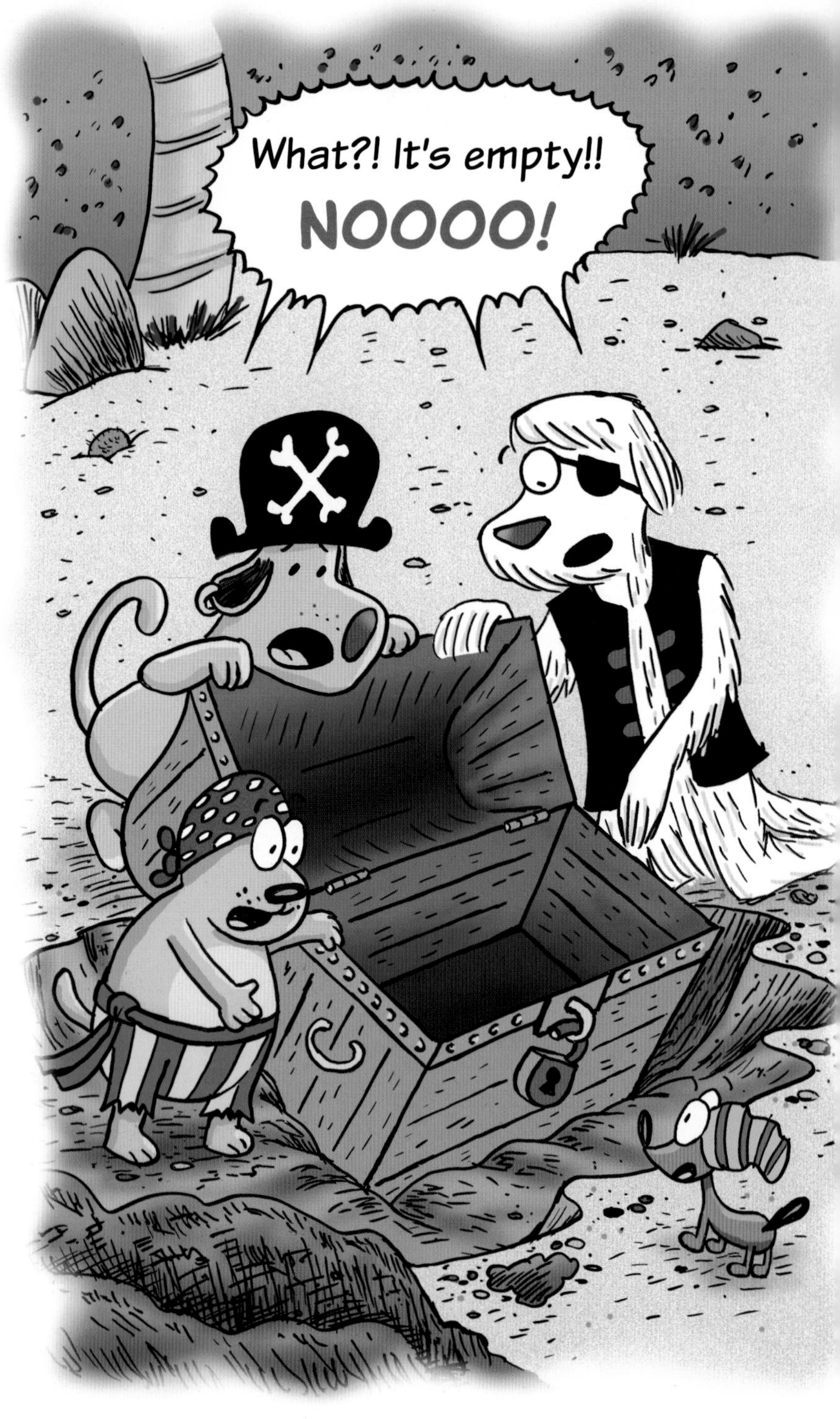
What?! It's empty!!
NOOOO!

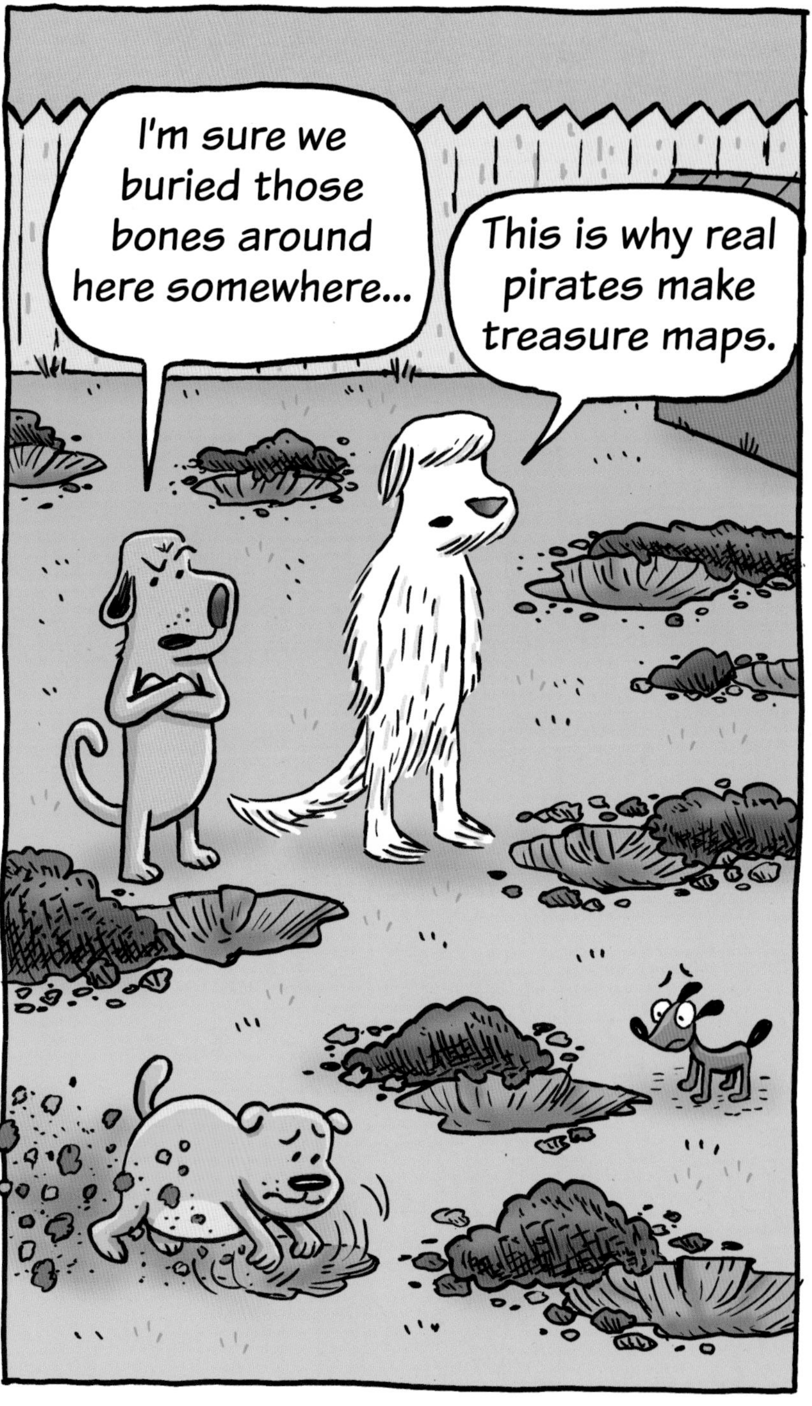
I'm sure we buried those bones around here somewhere...
This is why real pirates make treasure maps.

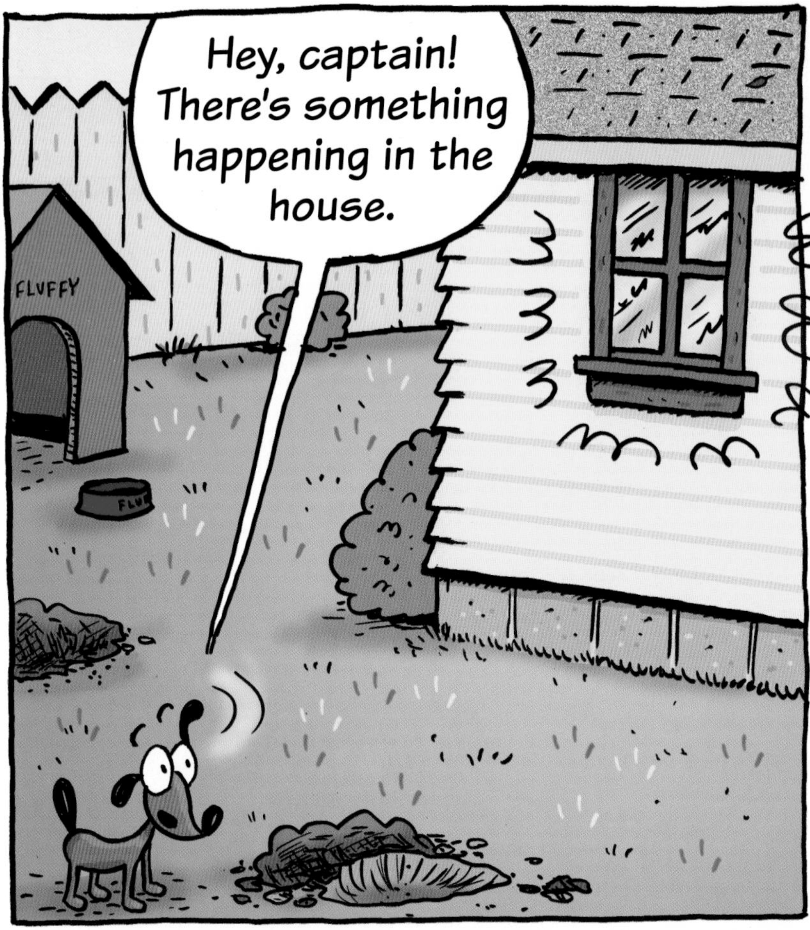
Hey, captain! There's something happening in the house.
FLUFFY

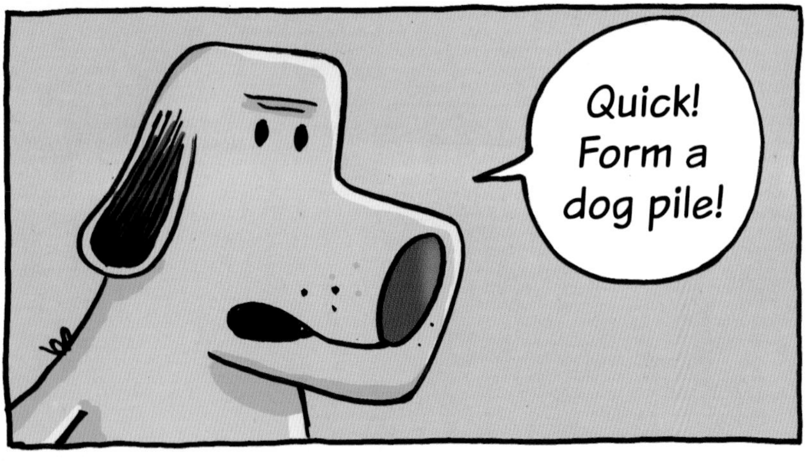
Quick! Form a dog pile!

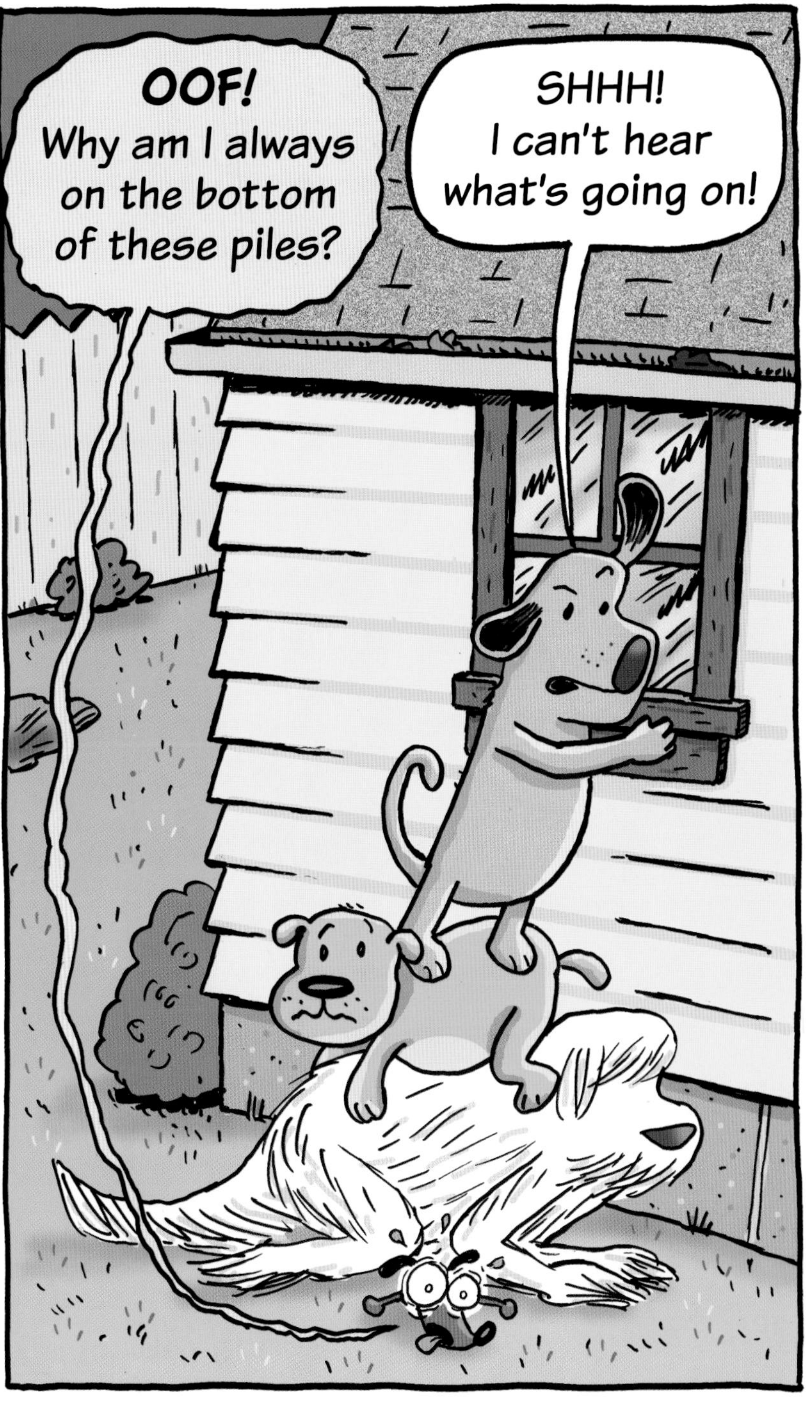
OOF! Why am I always on the bottom of these piles?
SHHH! I can't hear what's going on!

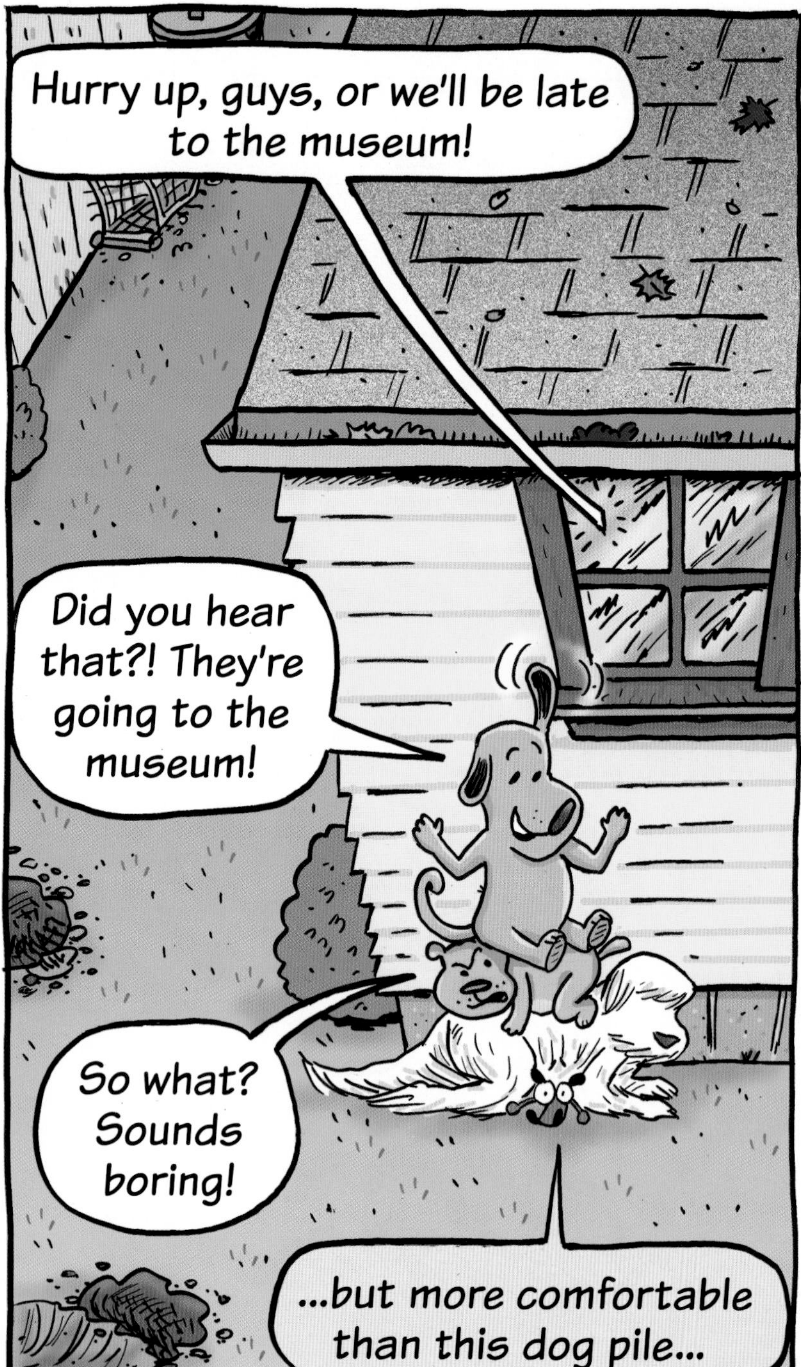
Hurry up, guys, or we'll be late to the museum!
Did you hear that?! They're going to the museum!
So what? Sounds boring!
...but more comfortable than this dog pile...

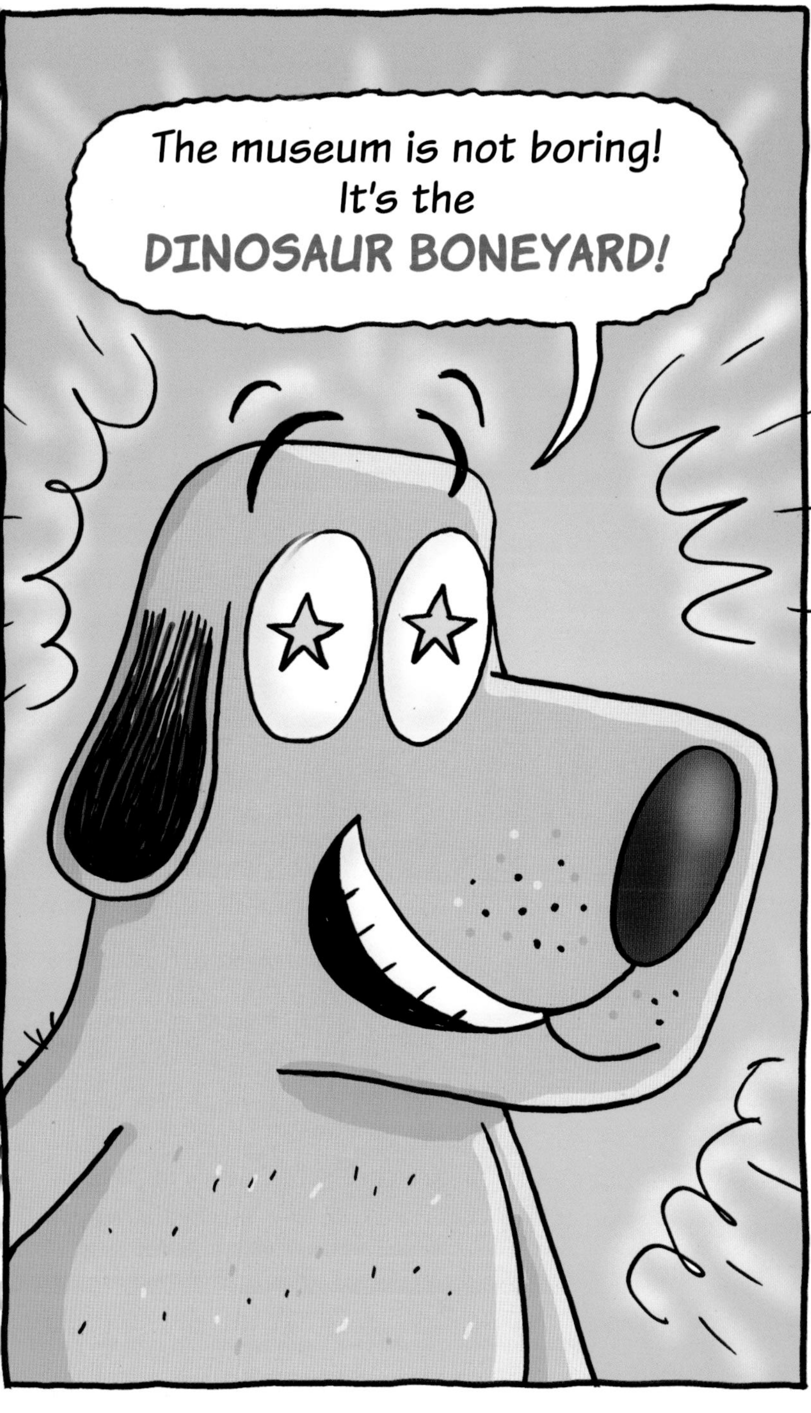
The museum is not boring! It's the DINOSAUR BONEYARD!

The Dinosaur Boneyard is the place where all of the dinosaurs went to die. The biggest, juiciest bones the world has ever seen are all together in one place, ripe for the picking!

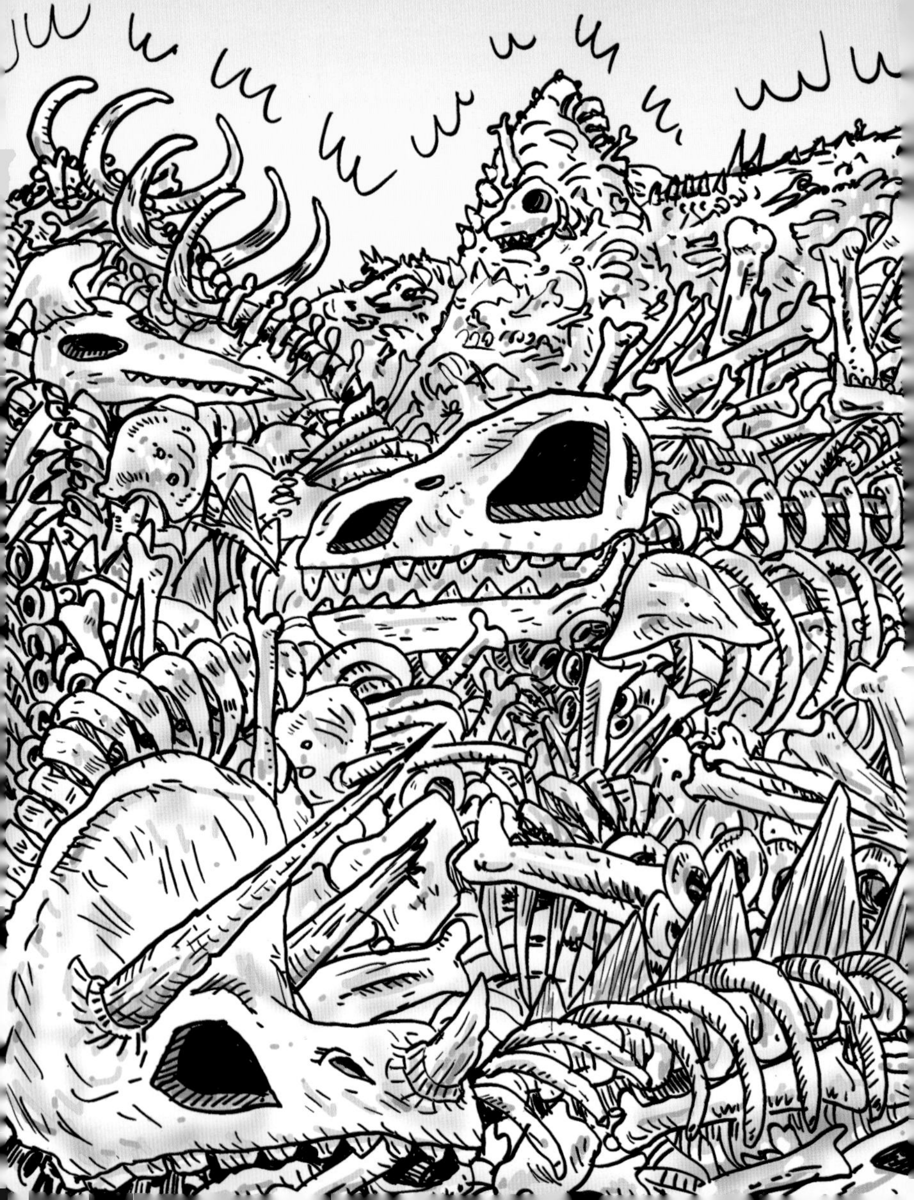

Chapter Two

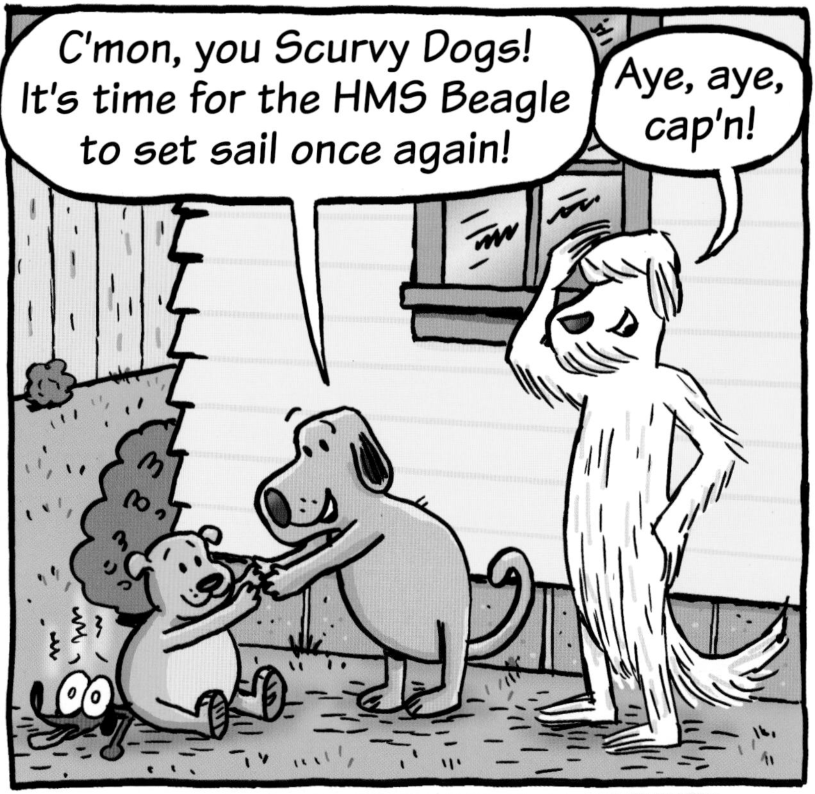

C'mon, you Scurvy Dogs! It's time for the HMS Beagle to set sail once again!
Aye, aye, cap'n!

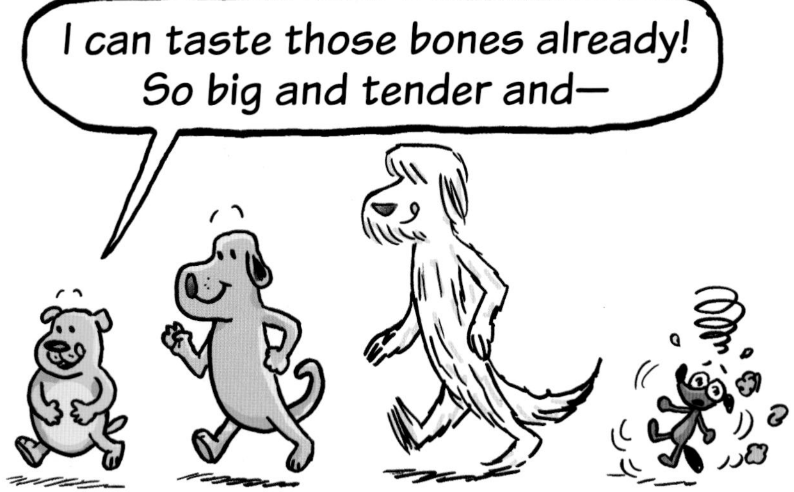

I can taste those bones already! So big and tender and—

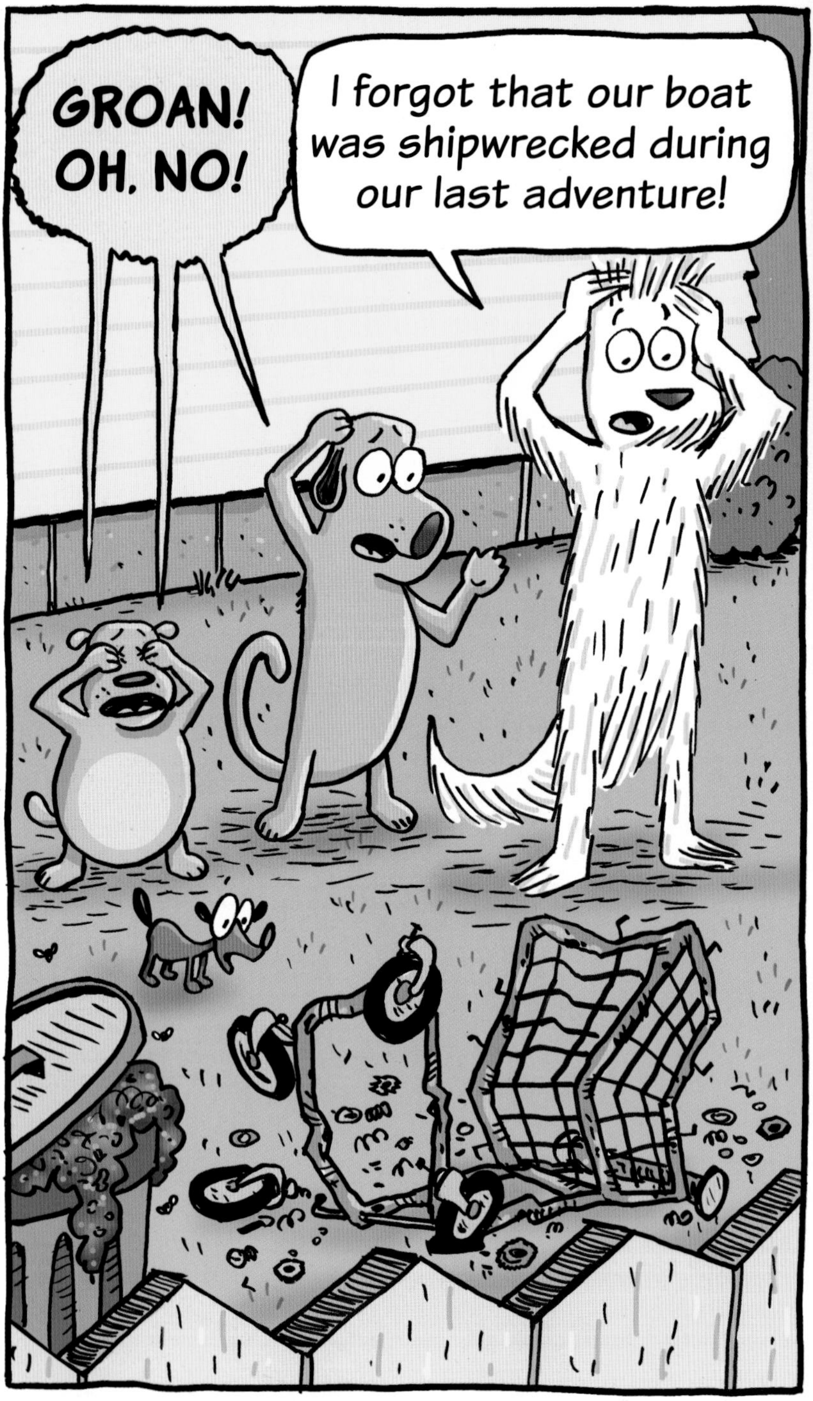
GROAN! OH, NO!
I forgot that our boat was shipwrecked during our last adventure!

The brave pirates stared at the broken remains of the HMS Beagle.

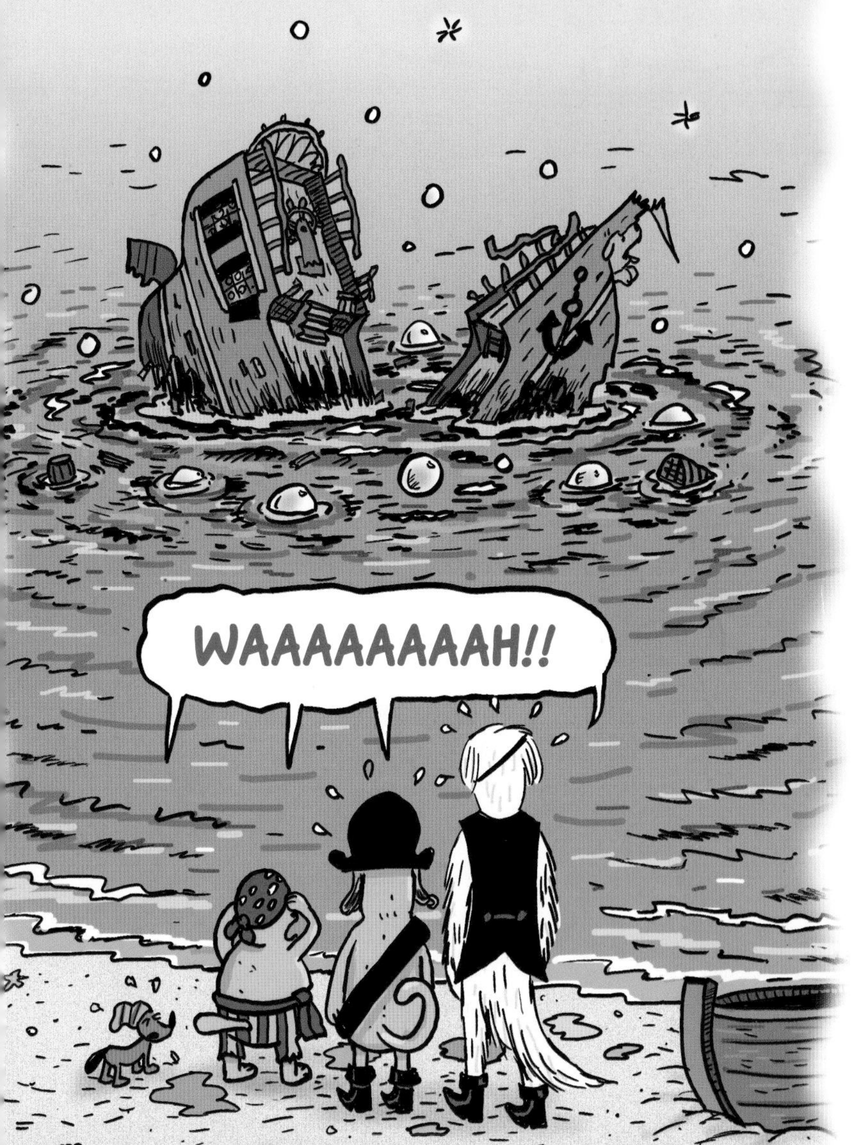
WAAAAAAAAH!!

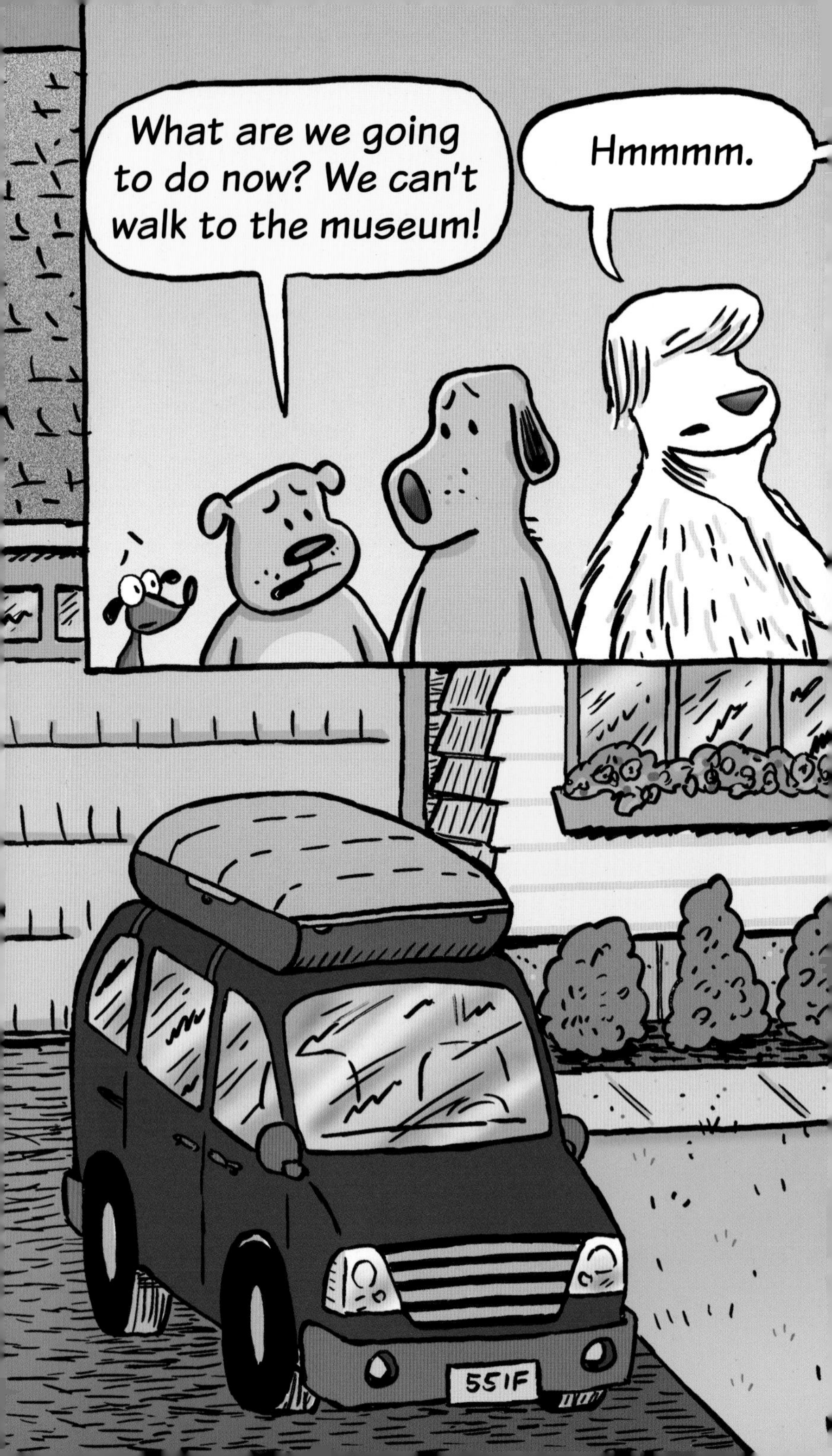
What are we going to do now? We can't walk to the museum!
Hmmmm.
551F

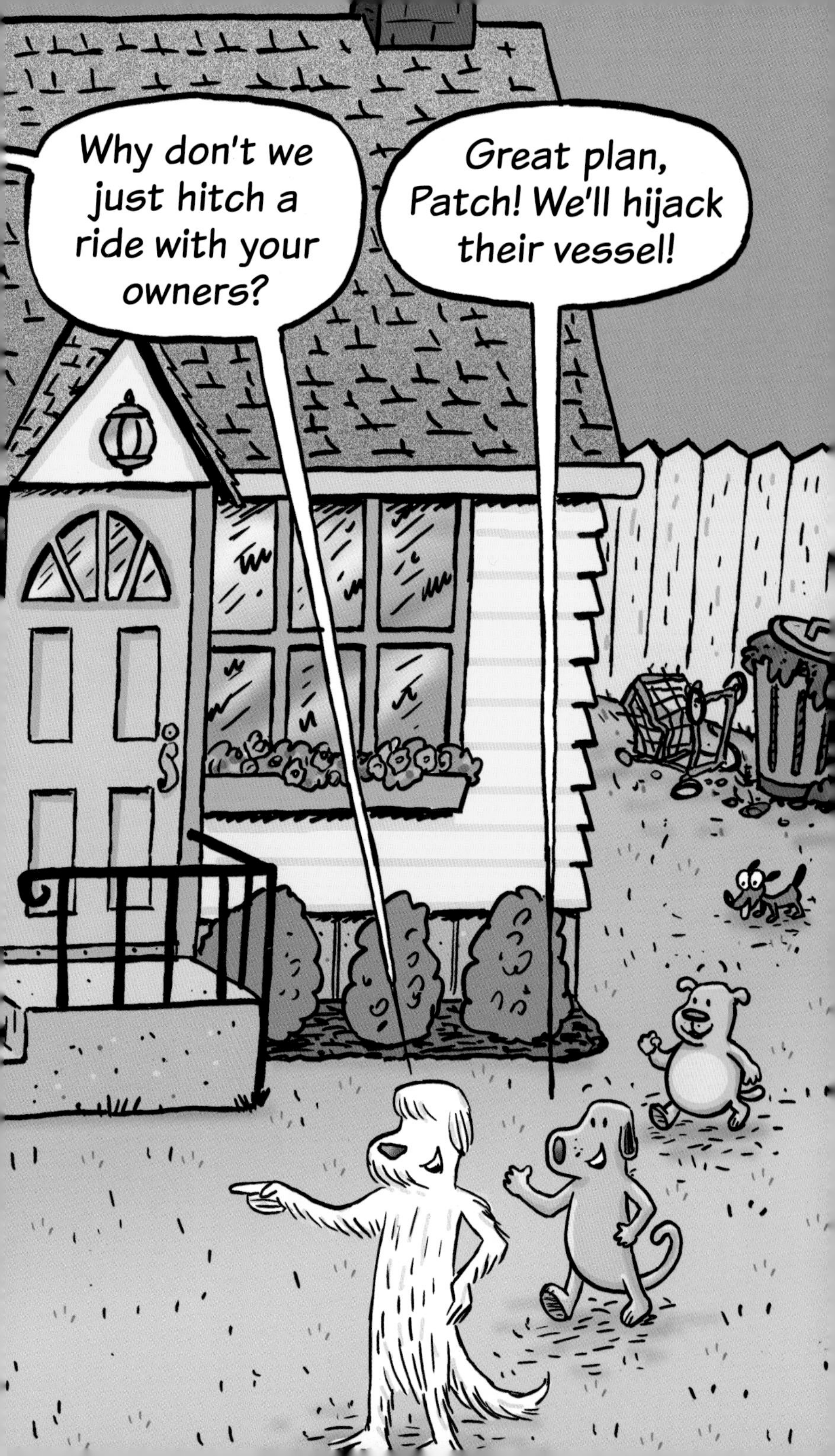
Why don't we just hitch a ride with your owners?
Great plan, Patch! We'll hijack their vessel!

The pirates spotted a beautiful new ship, just waiting to be plundered. Silently, they made their approach.

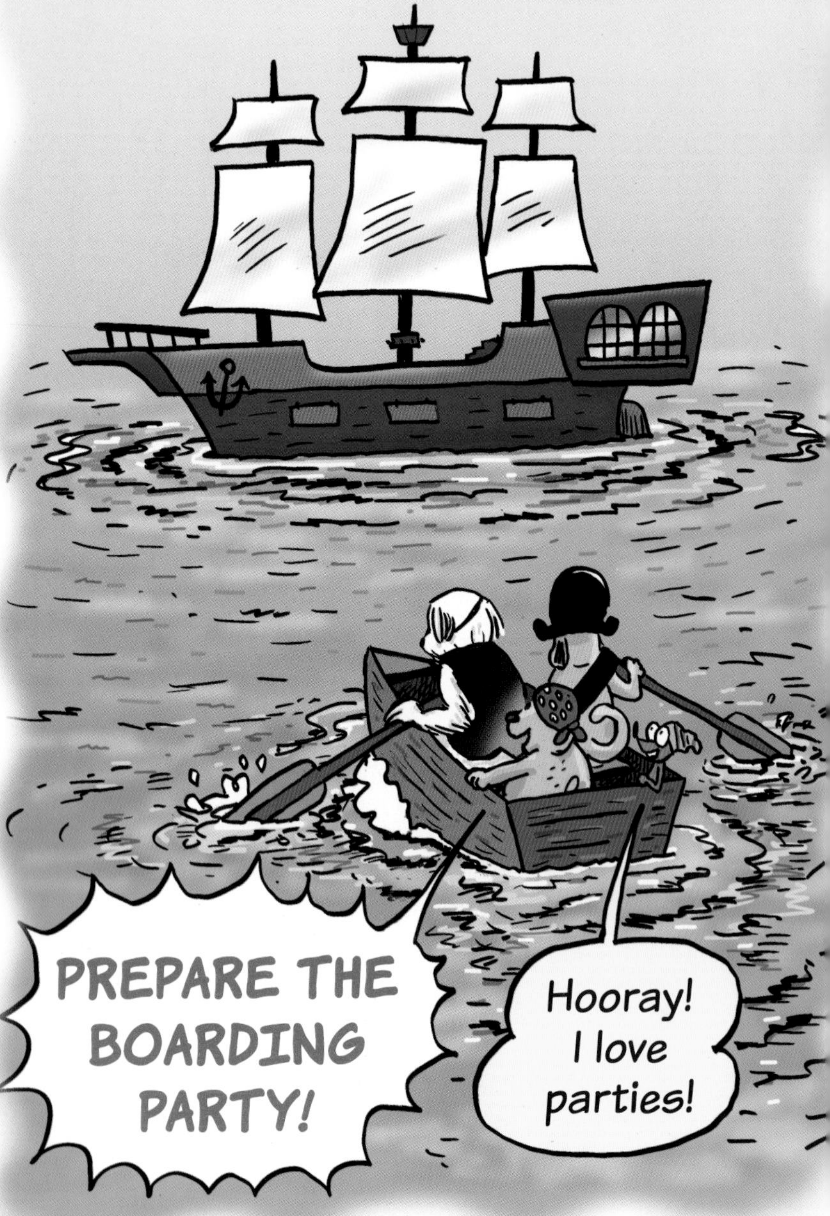
PREPARE THE BOARDING PARTY!
Hooray! I love parties!

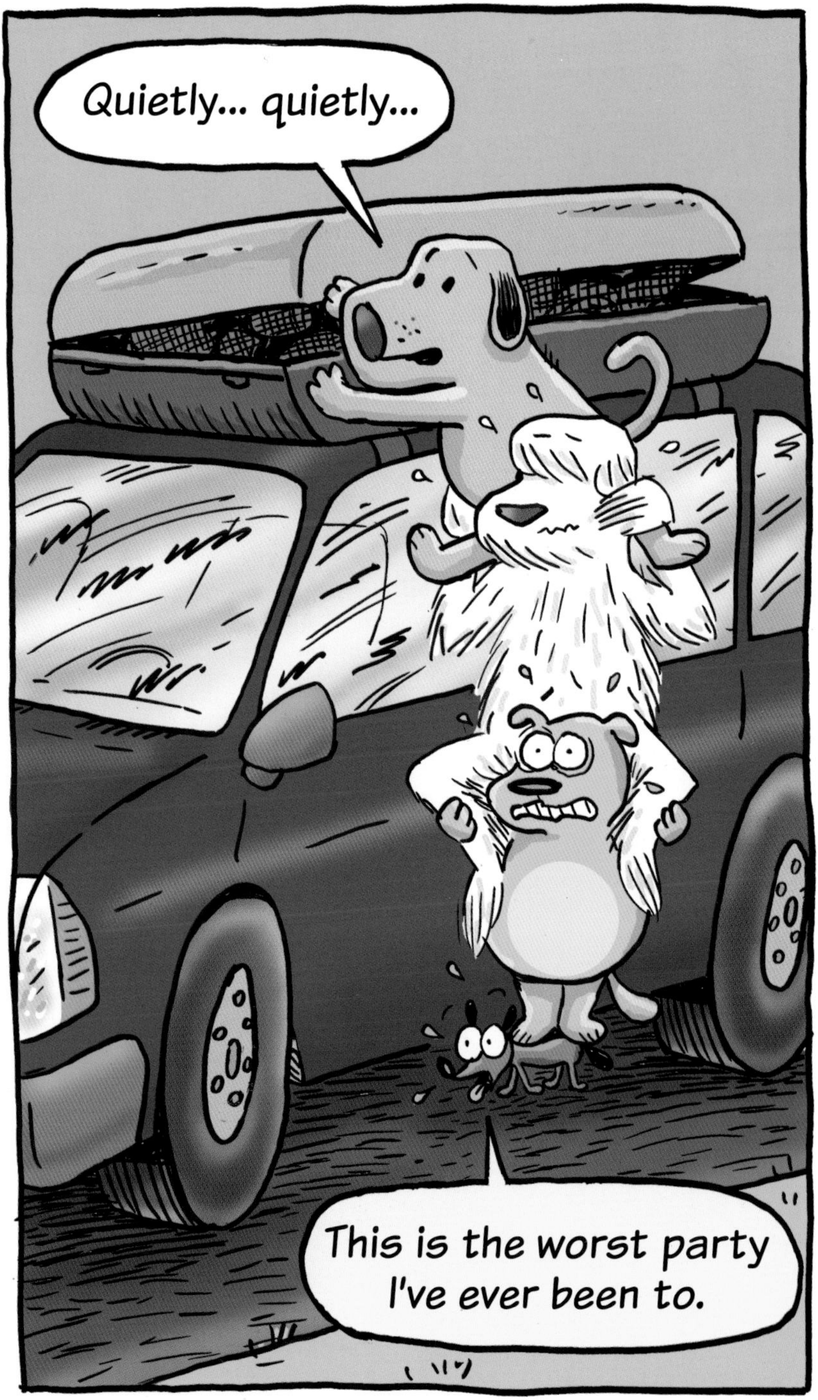
Quietly... quietly...
This is the worst party I've ever been to.

The fearsome foursome boarded the unsuspecting ship.

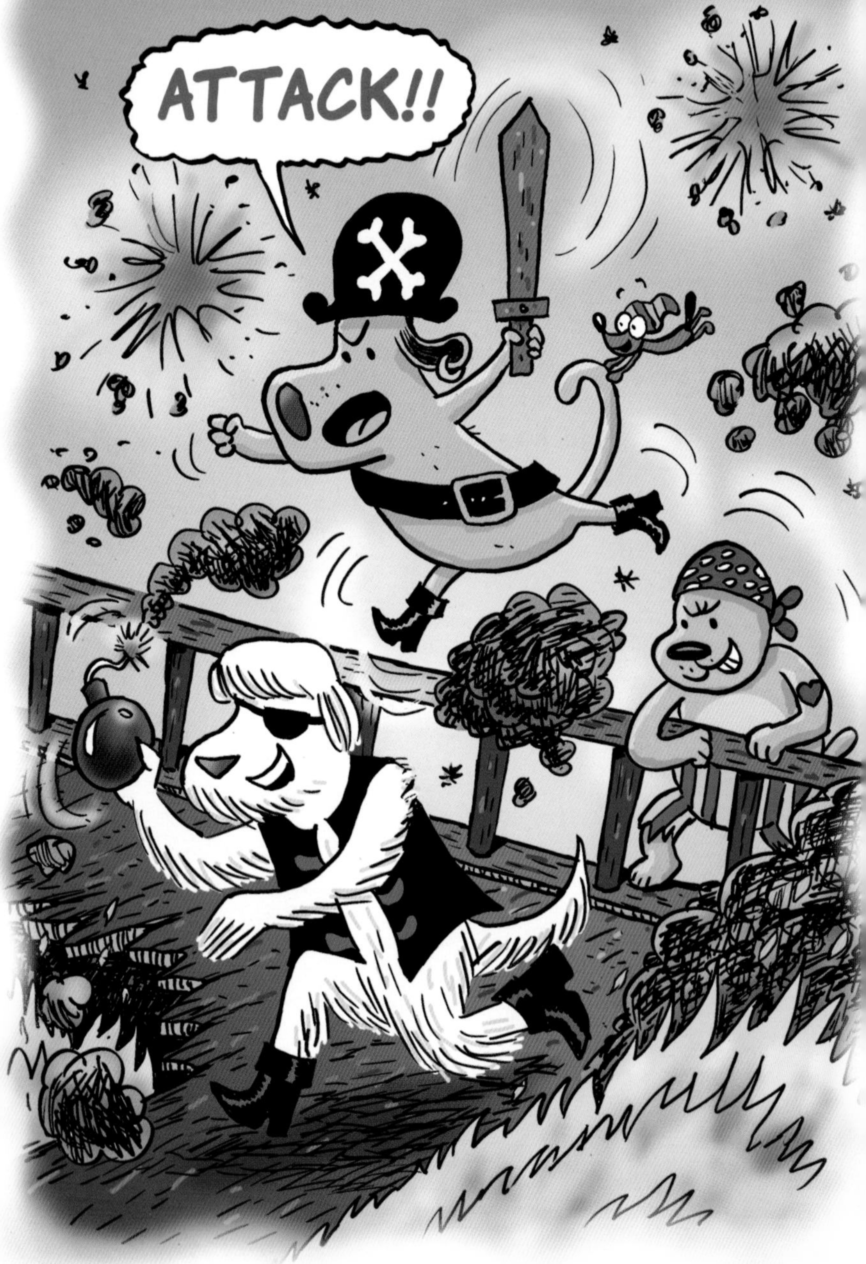
ATTACK!!

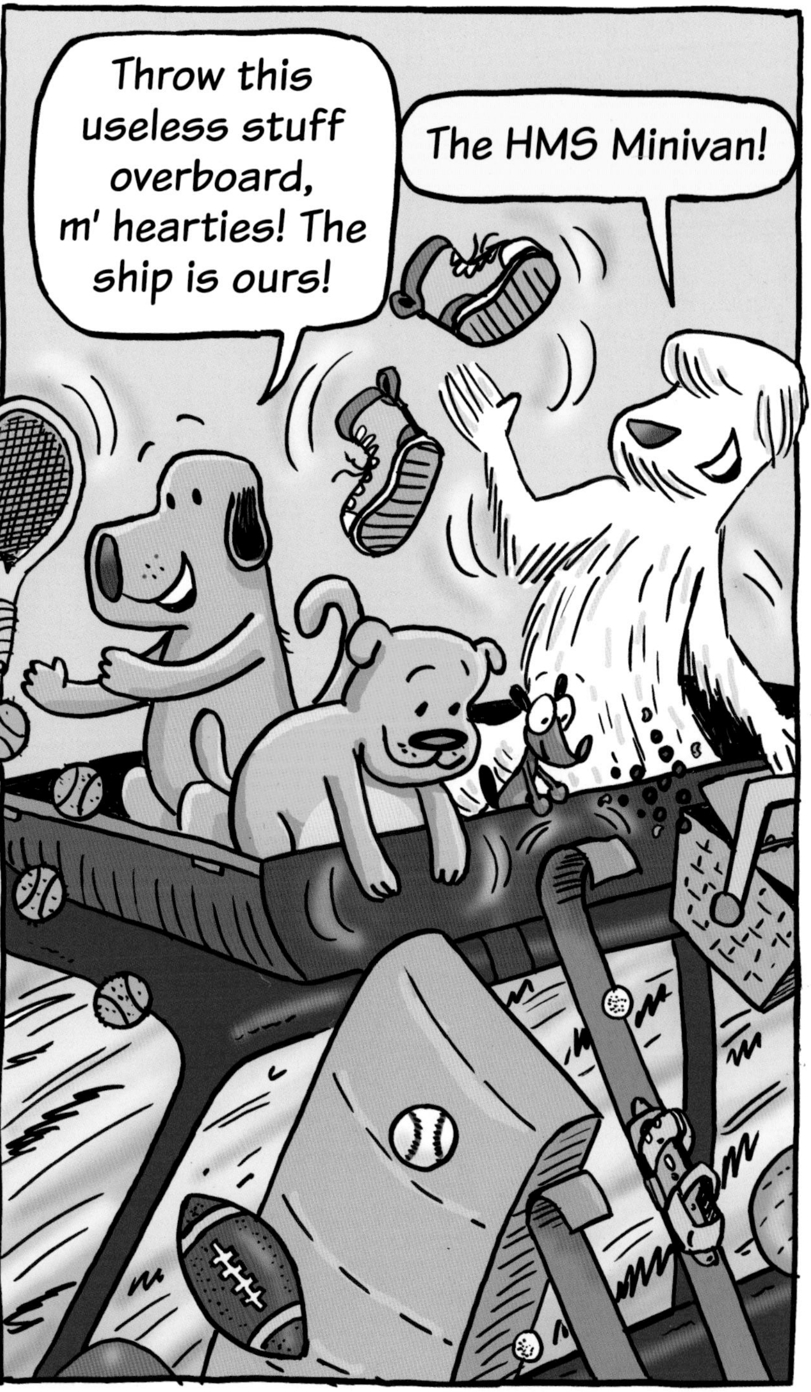
Throw this useless stuff overboard, m' hearties! The ship is ours!
The HMS Minivan!

The boarding party was a success, and now the Scurvy Dogs controlled a brand-new pirate ship.

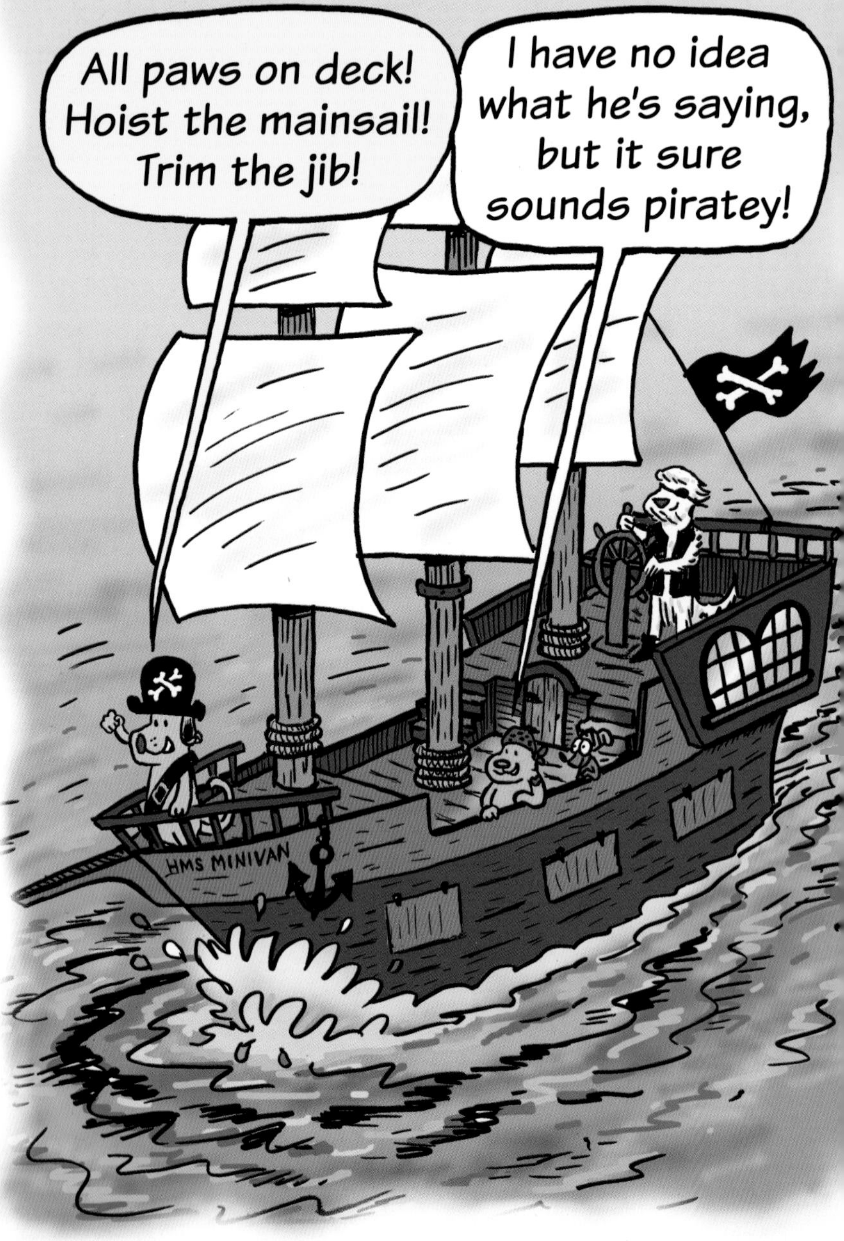
All paws on deck! Hoist the mainsail! Trim the jib!
I have no idea what he's saying, but it sure sounds piratey!
HMS MINIVAN

Chapter Three

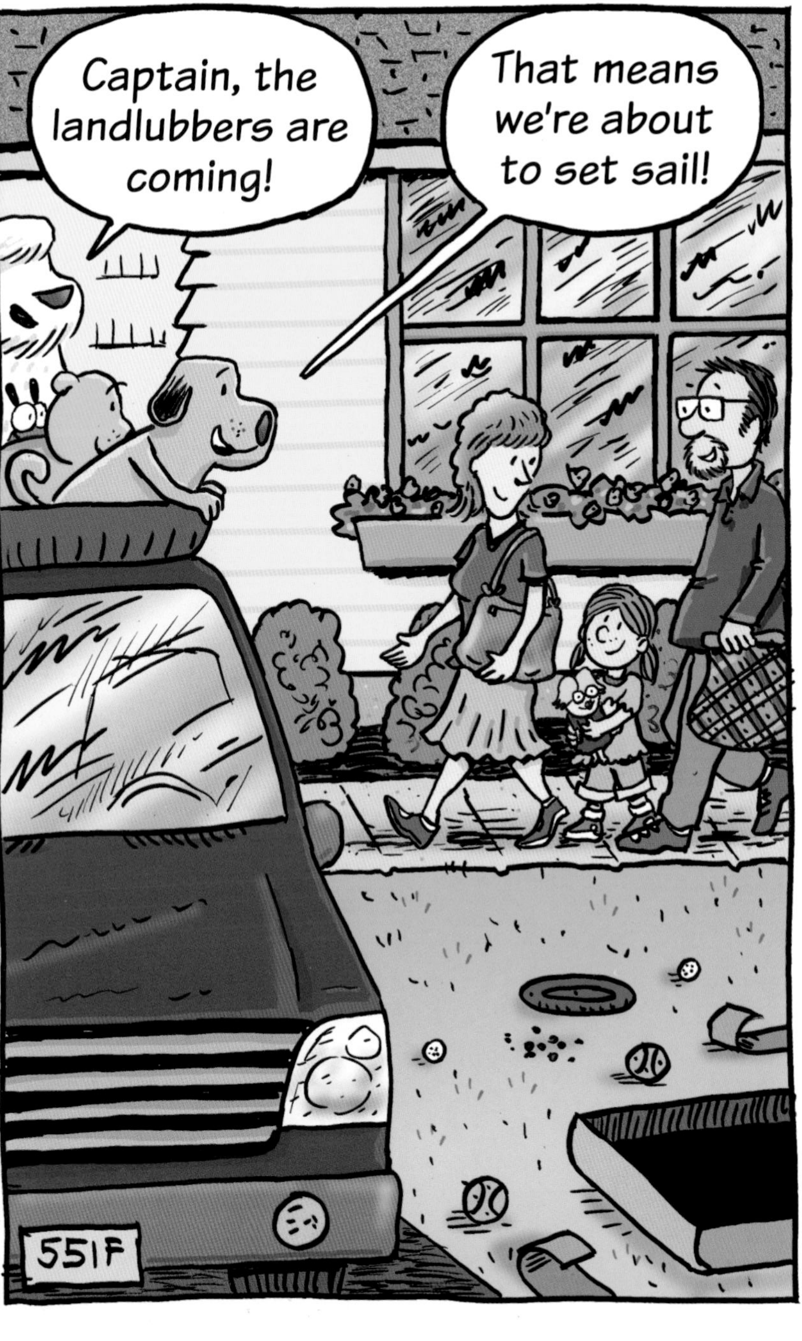
Captain, the landlubbers are coming!
That means we're about to set sail!
551F

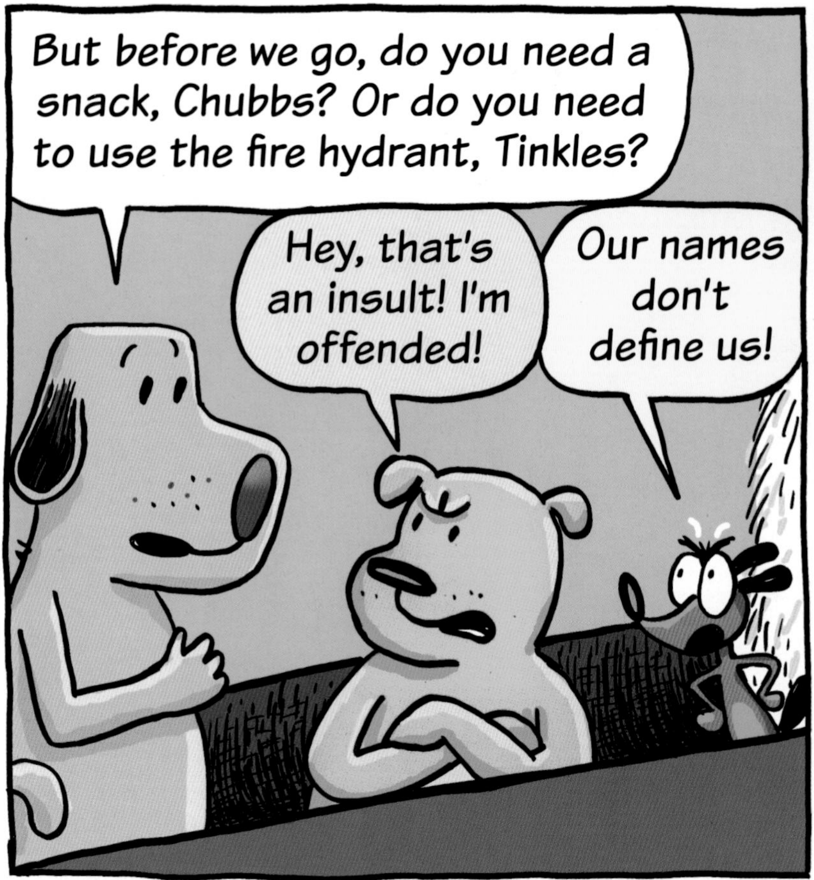
But before we go, do you need a snack, Chubbs? Or do you need to use the fire hydrant, Tinkles?
Hey, that's an insult! I'm offended!
Our names don't define us!

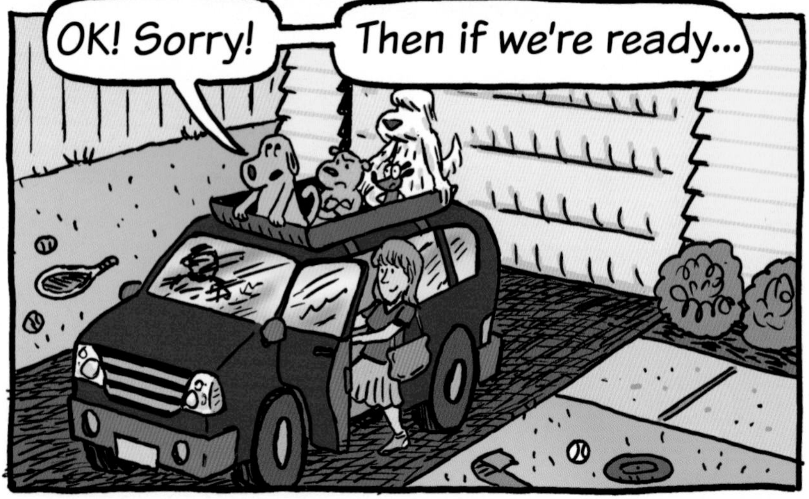
OK! Sorry!
Then if we're ready...

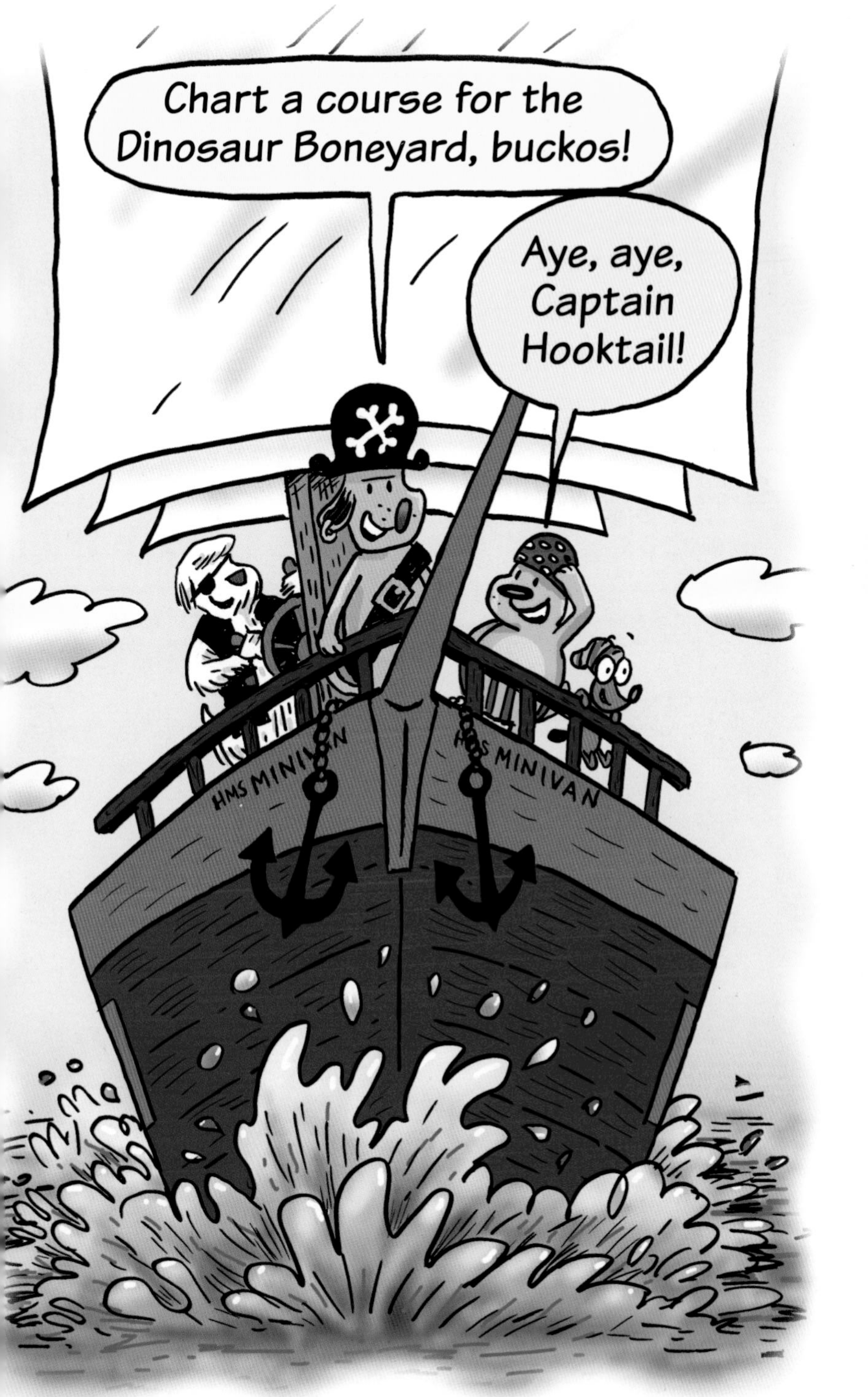

Chart a course for the Dinosaur Boneyard, buckos!
Aye, aye, Captain Hooktail!
HMS MINIVAN
HMS MINIVAN

The HMS Minivan sailed toward the museum.

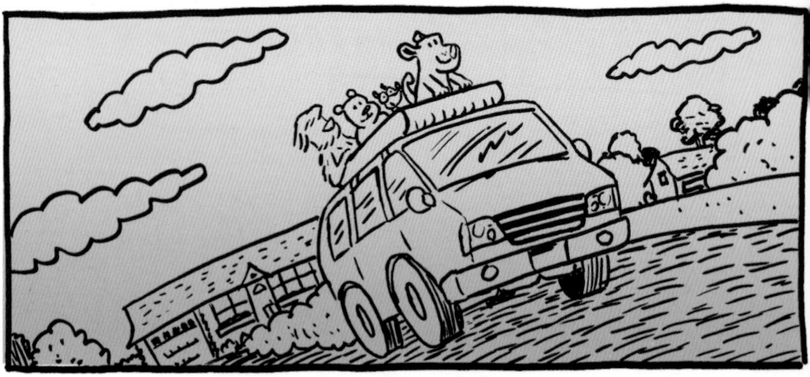

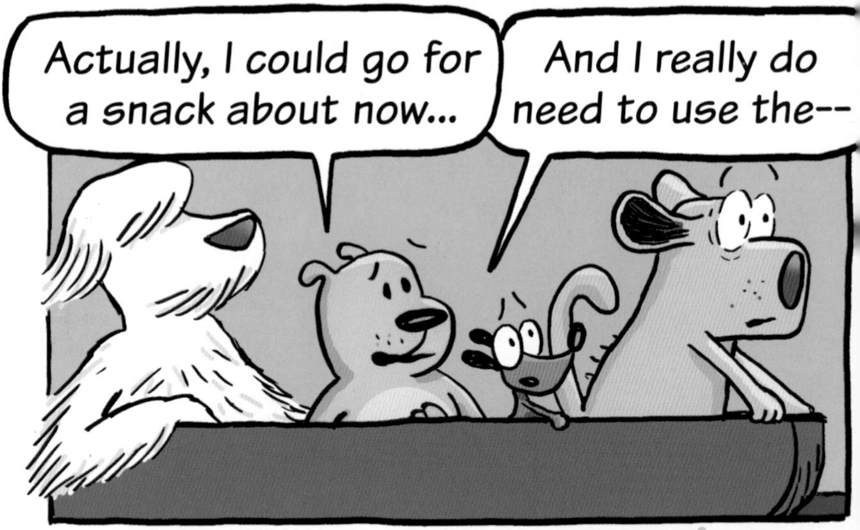
Actually, I could go for a snack about now...
And I really do need to use the--

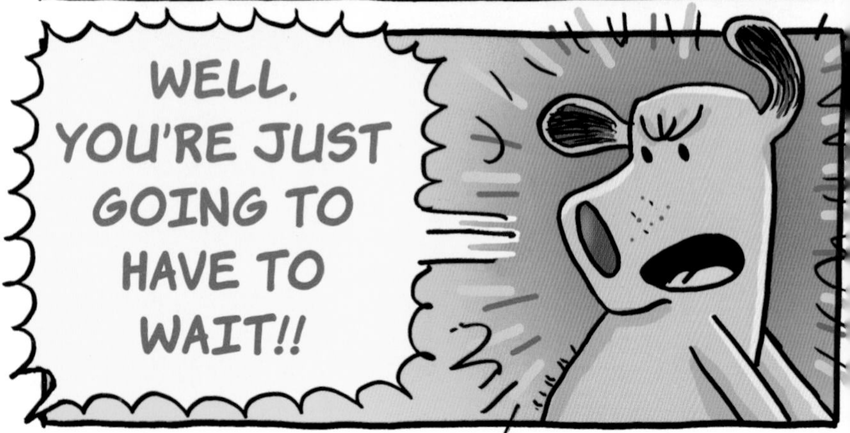
WELL, YOU'RE JUST GOING TO HAVE TO WAIT!!

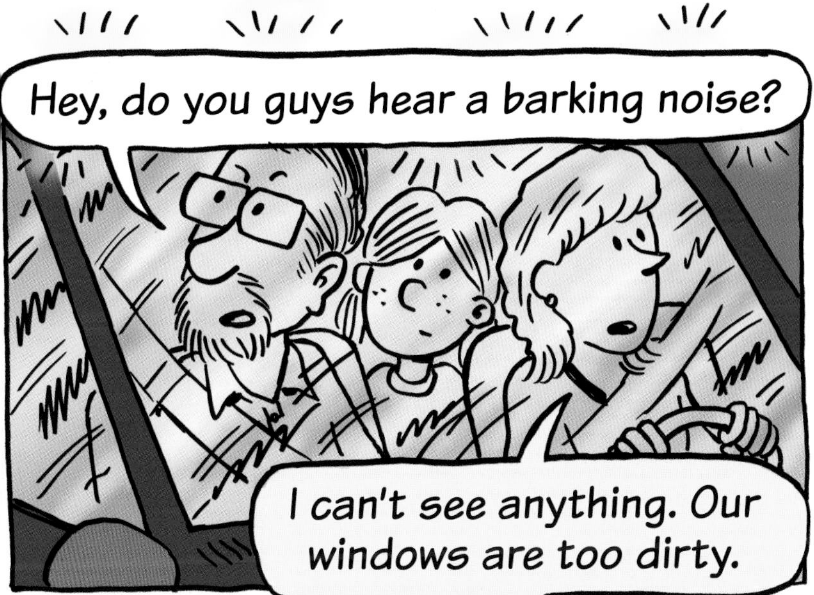
Hey, do you guys hear a barking noise?
I can't see anything. Our windows are too dirty.
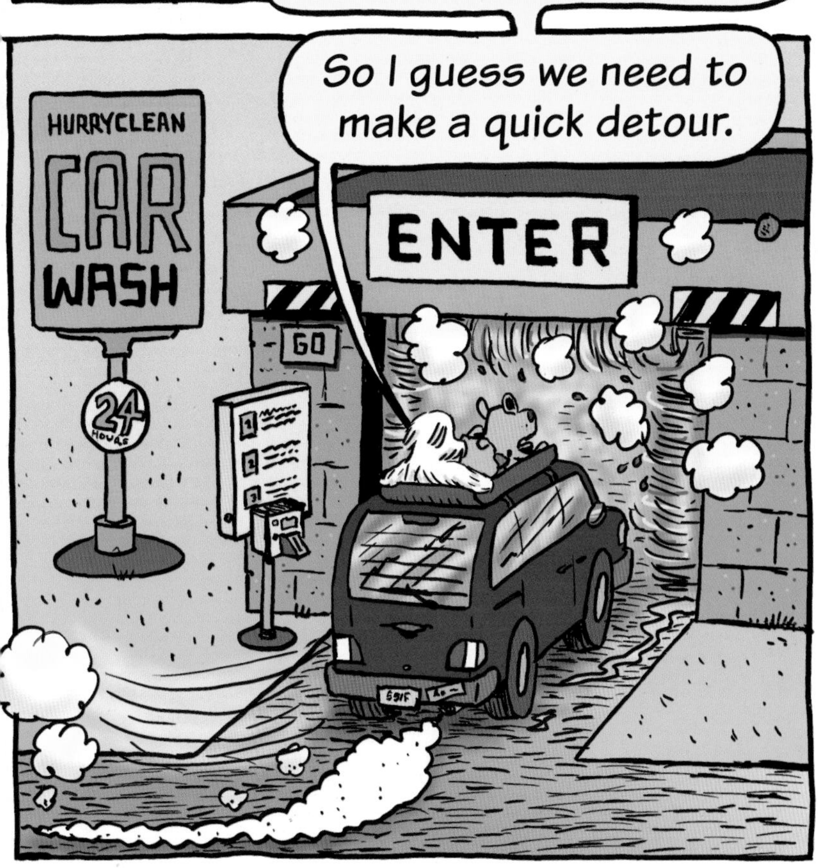
So I guess we need to make a quick detour.
HURRYCLEAN
CAR
WASH
24 HOURS
ENTER
GO

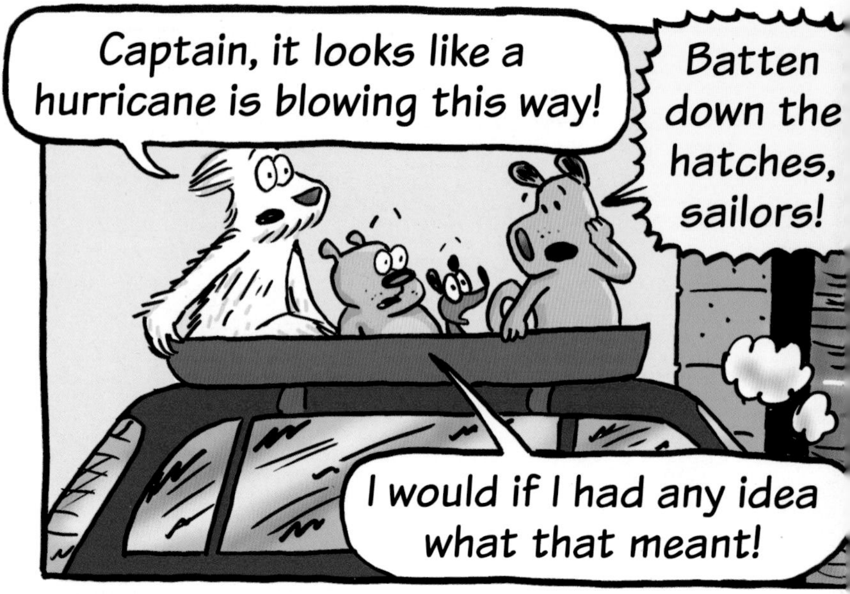
Captain, it looks like a hurricane is blowing this way!
Batten down the hatches, sailors!
I would if I had any idea what that meant!

A hurricane appeared out of nowhere and blasted the ship!

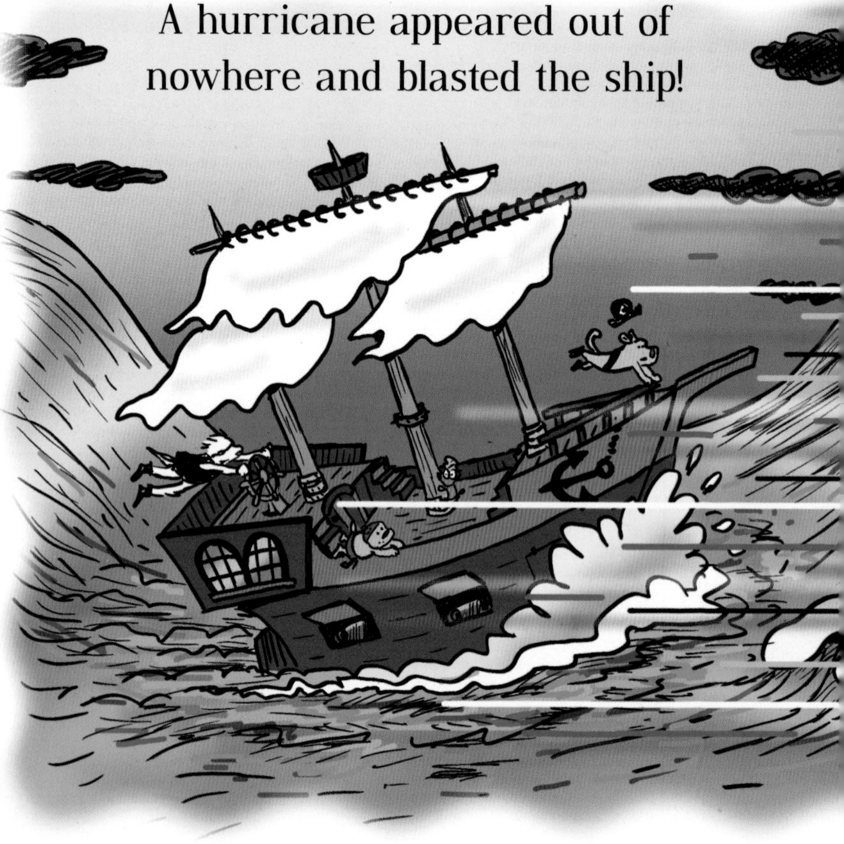

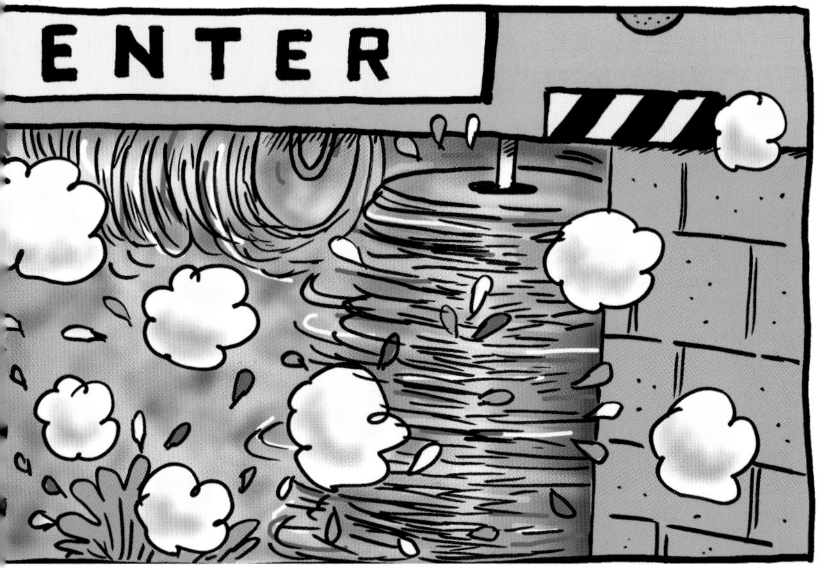
ENTER

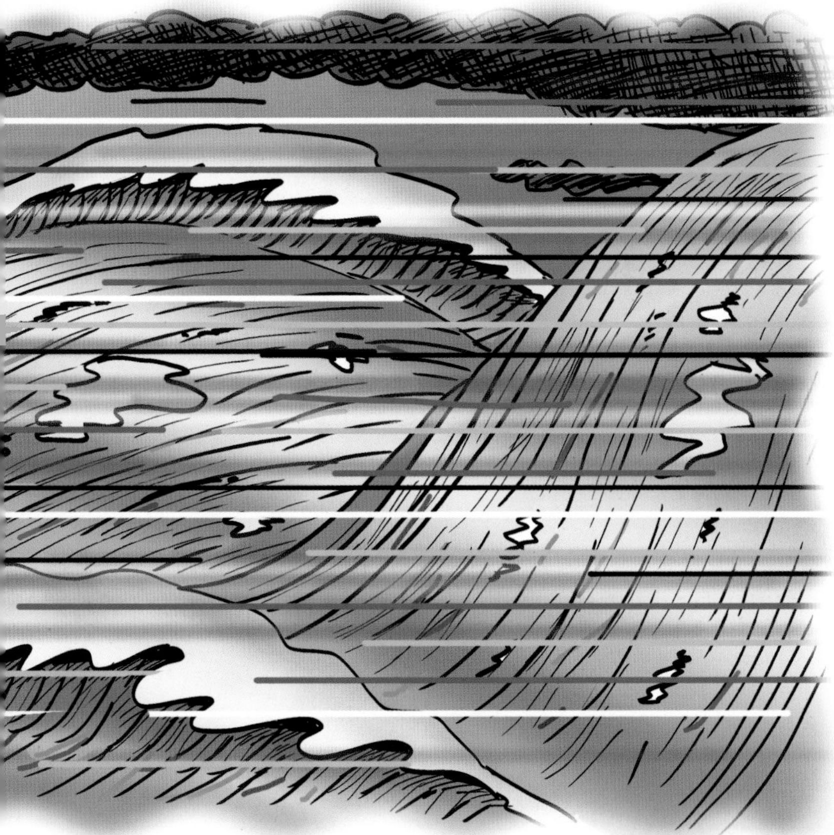

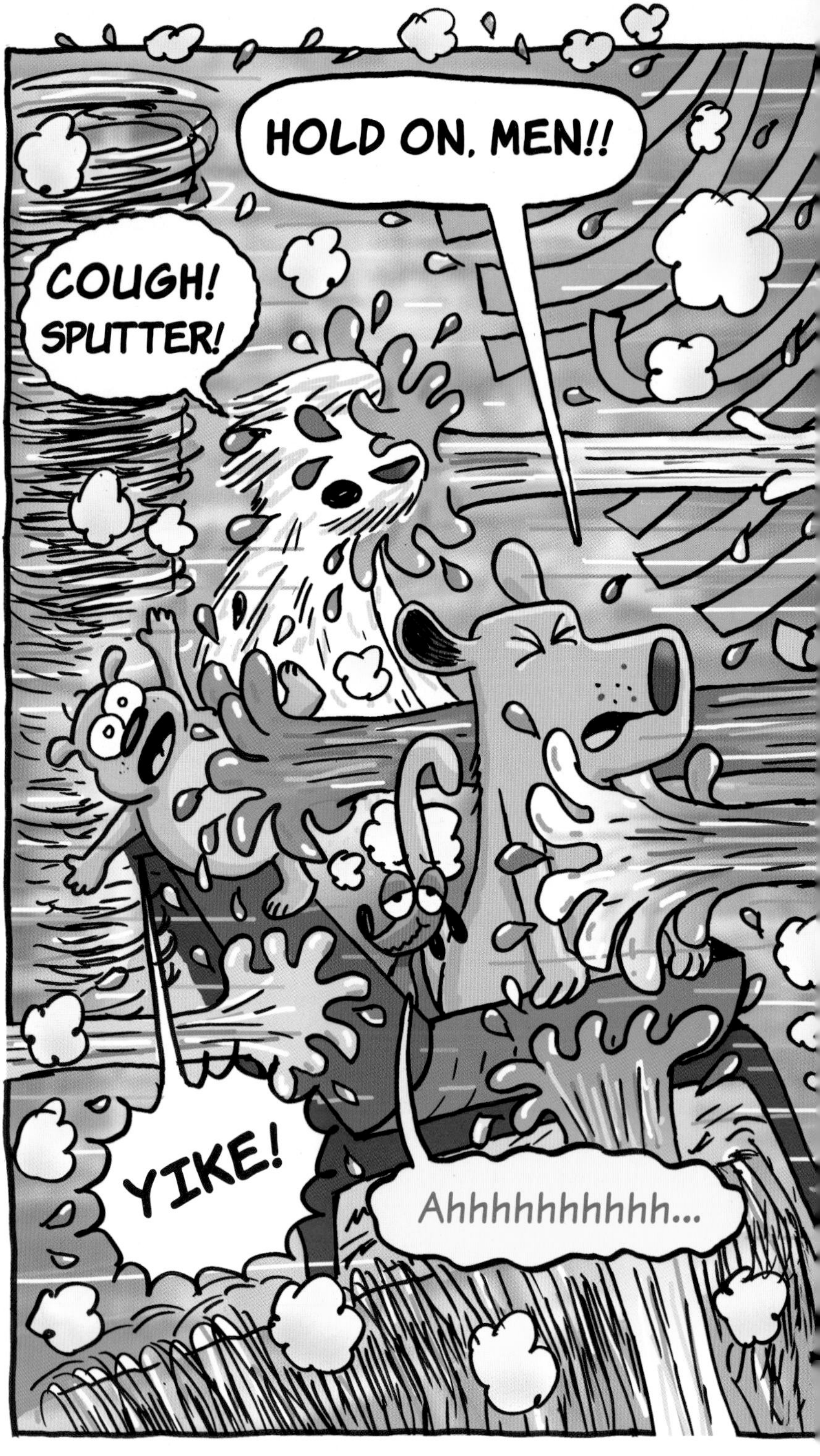
HOLD ON, MEN!!
COUGH! SPUTTER!
YIKE!
Ahhhhhhhhhh...

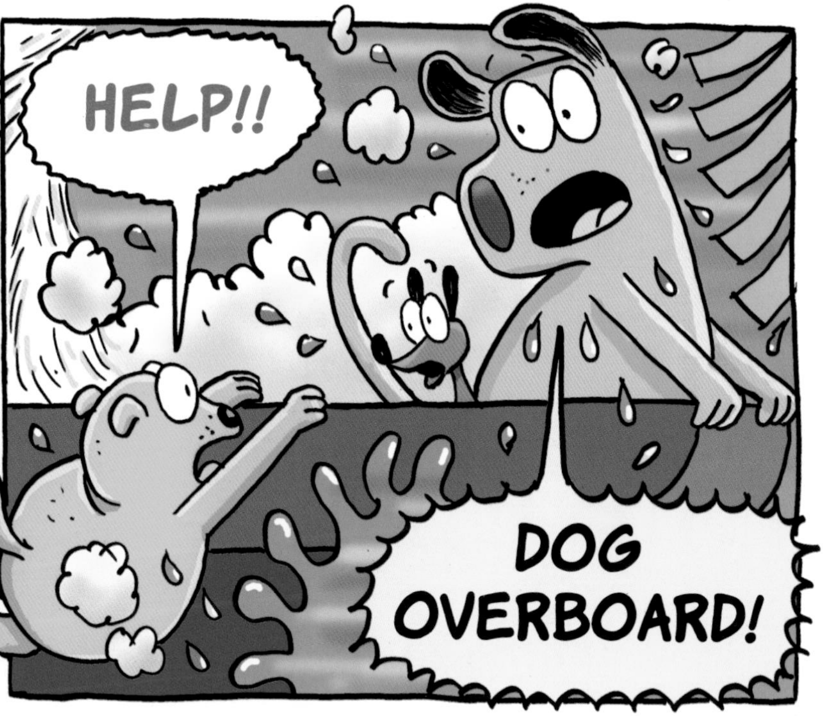
HELP!!
DOG OVERBOARD!

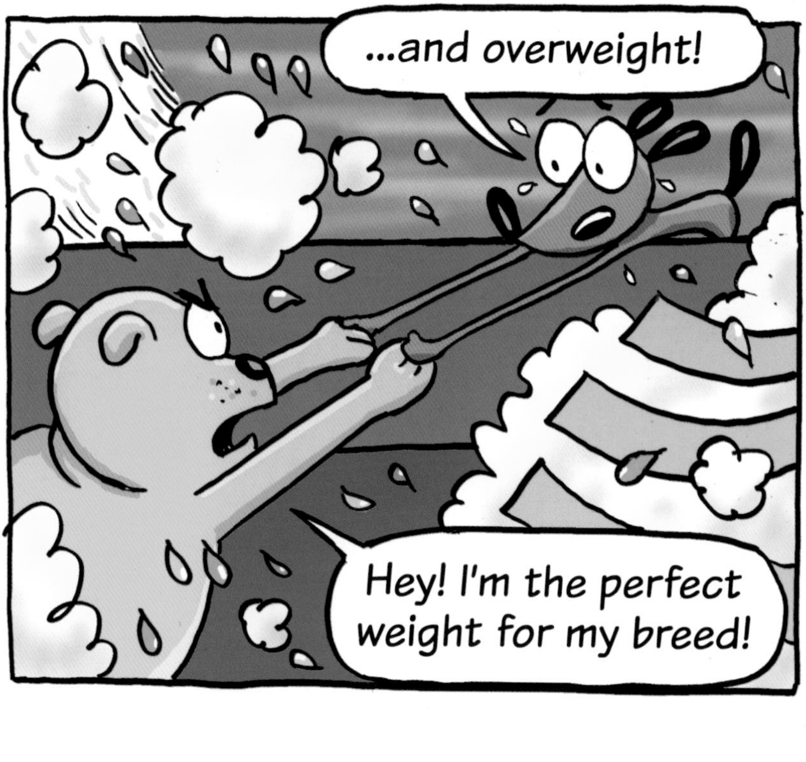
...and overweight!
Hey! I'm the perfect weight for my breed!

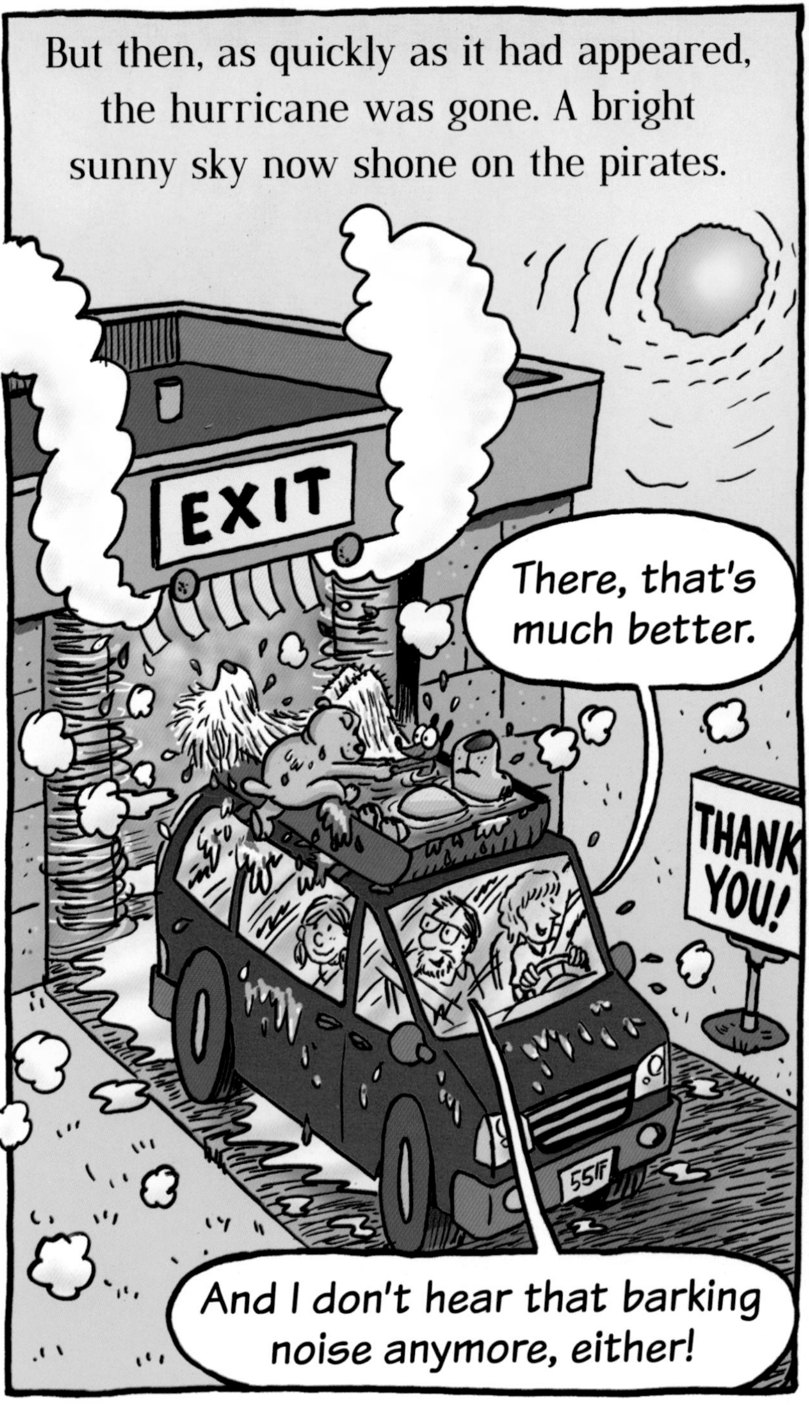
But then, as quickly as it had appeared, the hurricane was gone. A bright sunny sky now shone on the pirates.
EXIT
There, that's much better.
THANK YOU!
55IF
And I don't hear that barking noise anymore, either!

Chapter Four

The storm was behind them as the Scurvy crew sailed onward toward their tasty destination.

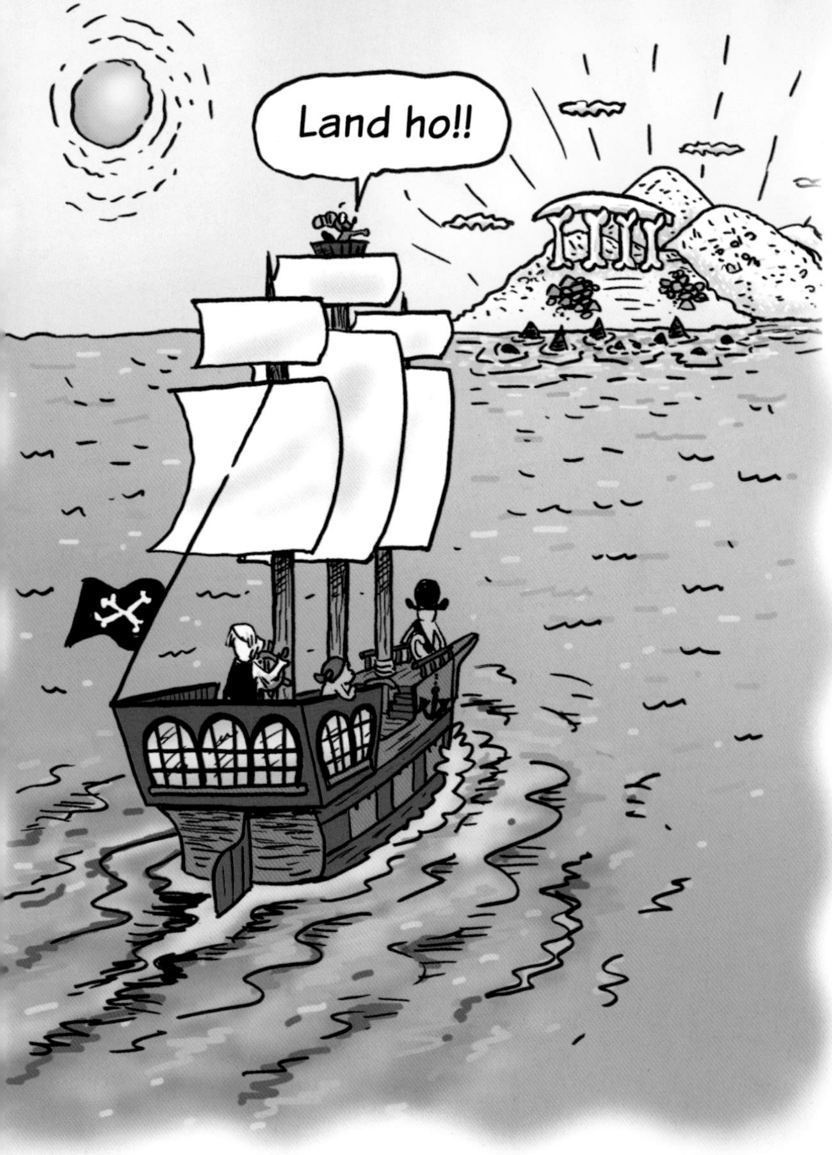
Land ho!!

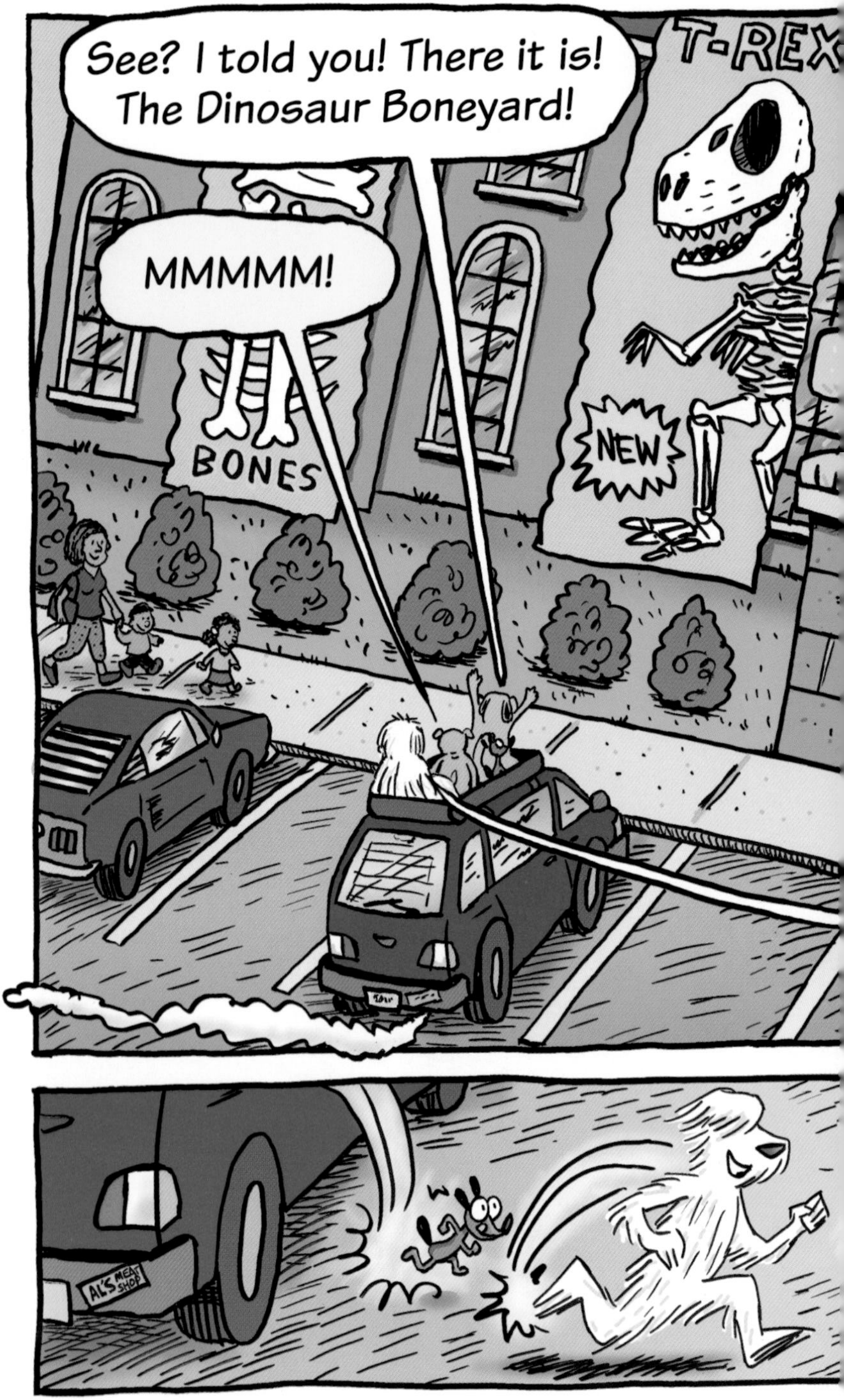
See? I told you! There it is! The Dinosaur Boneyard!
MMMMM!
T-REX
BONES
NEW
AL'S MEAT SHOP

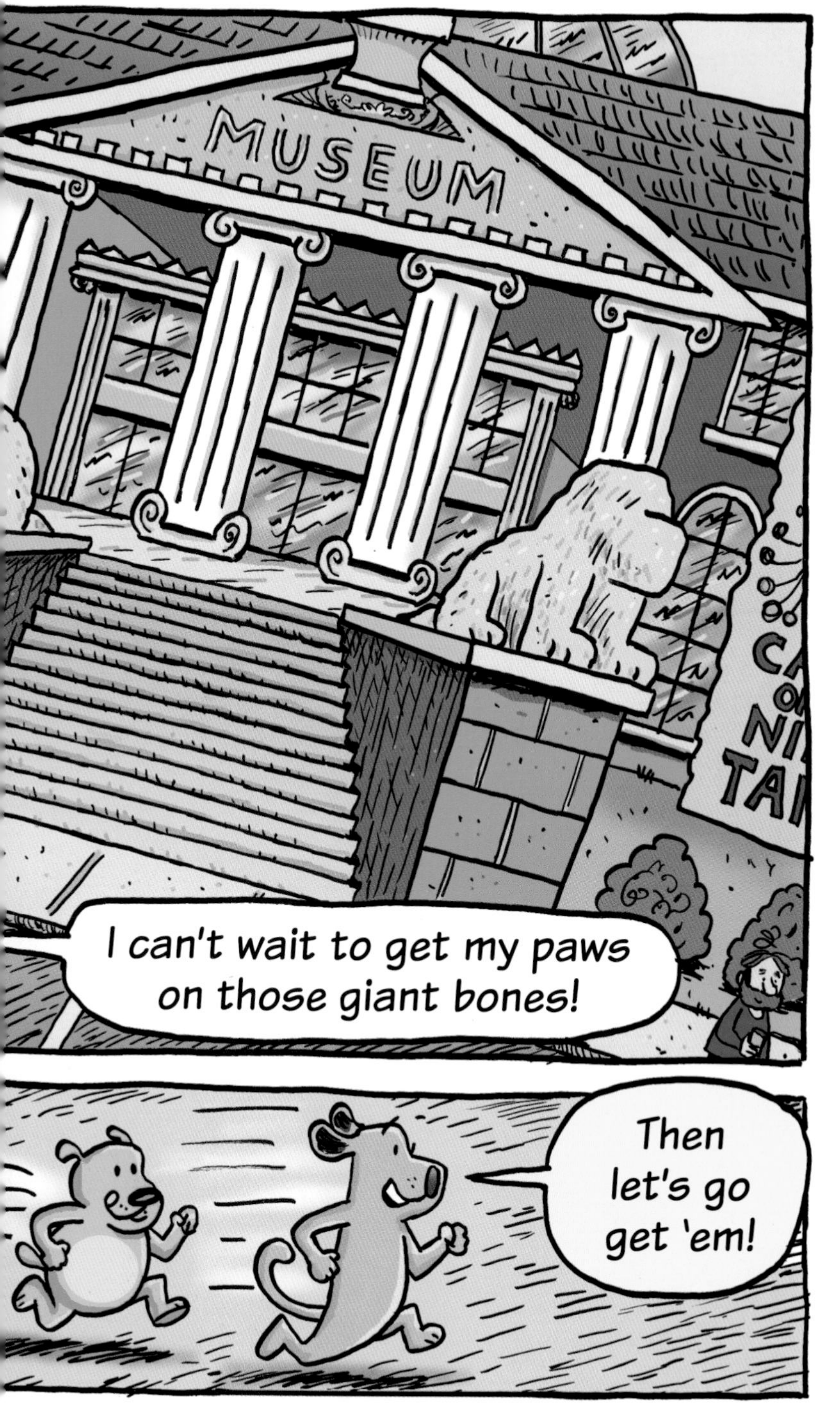
MUSEUM
I can't wait to get my paws on those giant bones!
Then let's go get 'em!

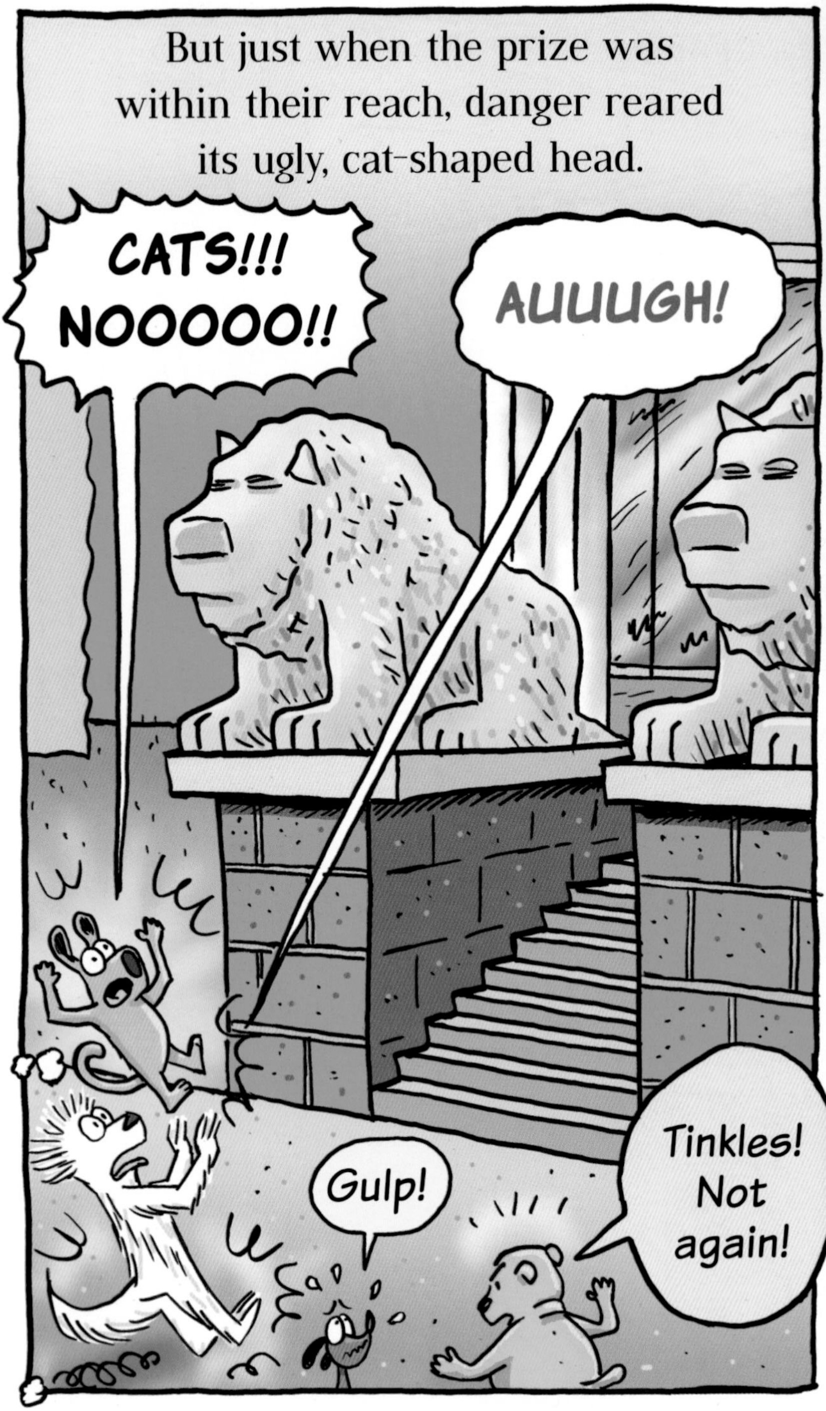
But just when the prize was within their reach, danger reared its ugly, cat-shaped head.
CATS!!! NOOOOO!!
AUUUGH!
Gulp!
Tinkles! Not again!

Giant rock cats guarded the entrance to the Dinosaur Boneyard!

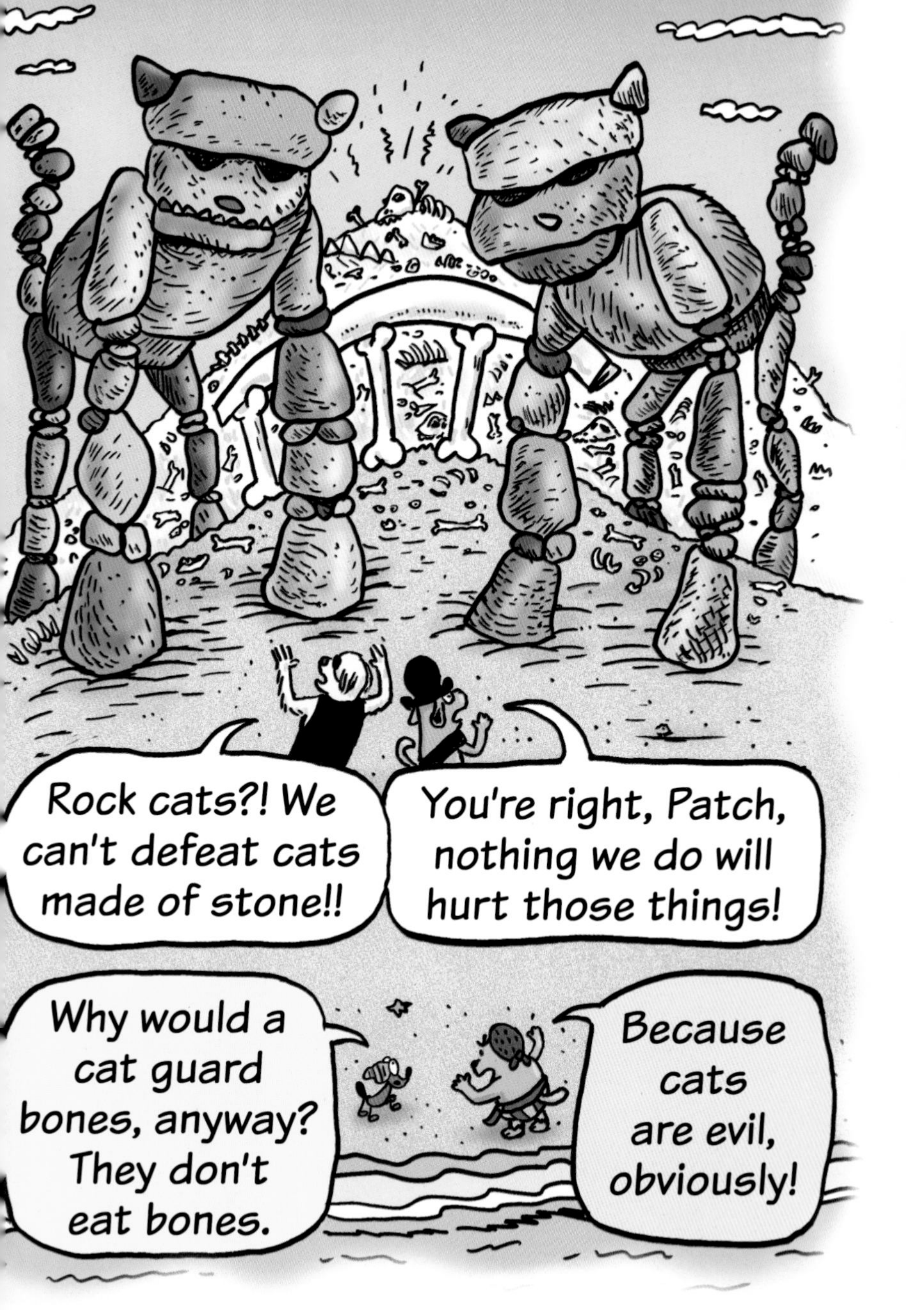
Rock cats?! We can't defeat cats made of stone!!
You're right, Patch, nothing we do will hurt those things!
Why would a cat guard bones, anyway? They don't eat bones.
Because cats are evil, obviously!

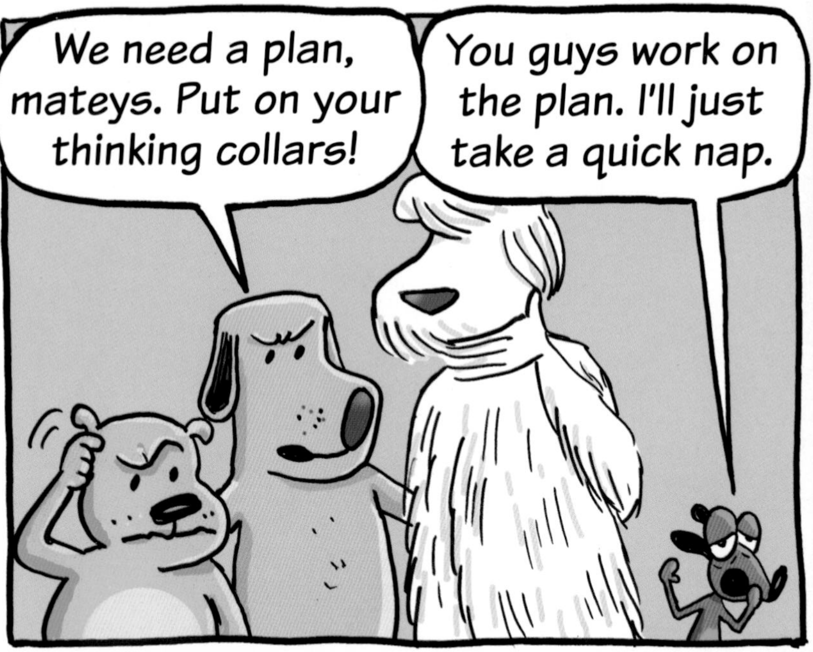
We need a plan, mateys. Put on your thinking collars!
You guys work on the plan. I'll just take a quick nap.

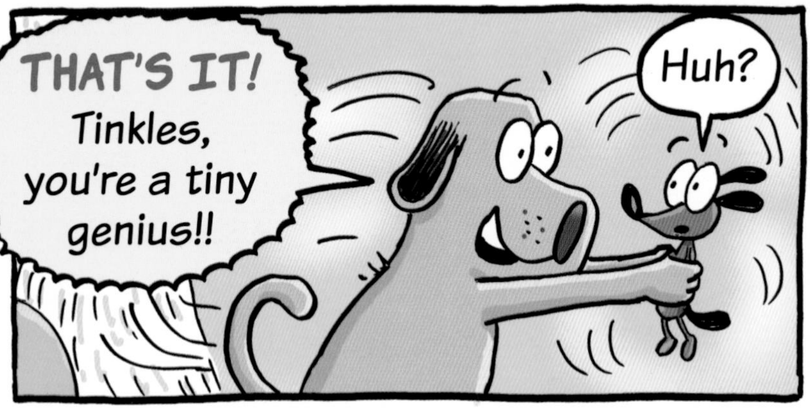
THAT'S IT! Tinkles, you're a tiny genius!!
Huh?

We'll lull those stony giants to sleep with a song! C'mon! Let's sing them a pirate lullaby!

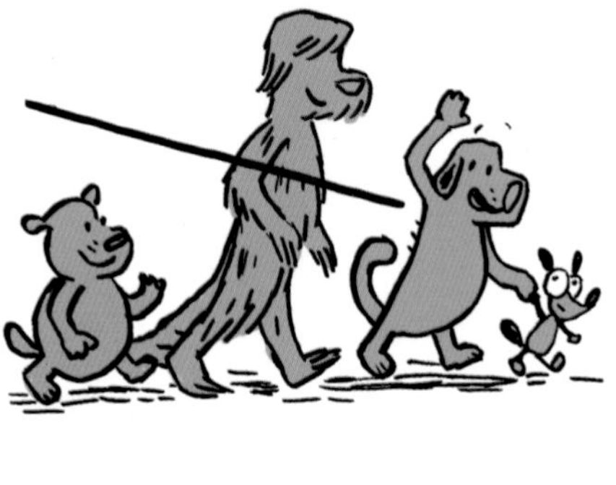

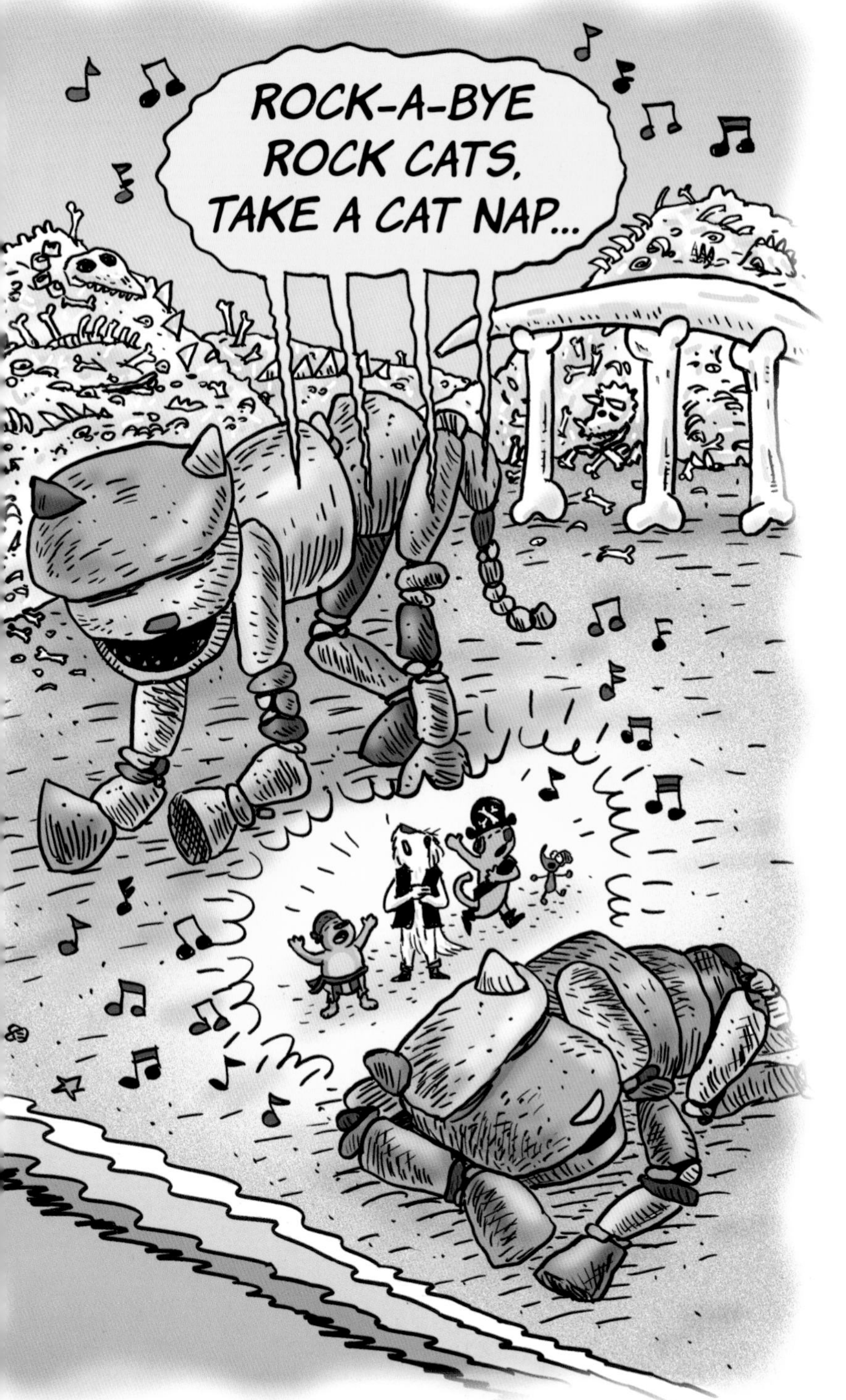
ROCK-A-BYE
ROCK CATS,
TAKE A CAT NAP...

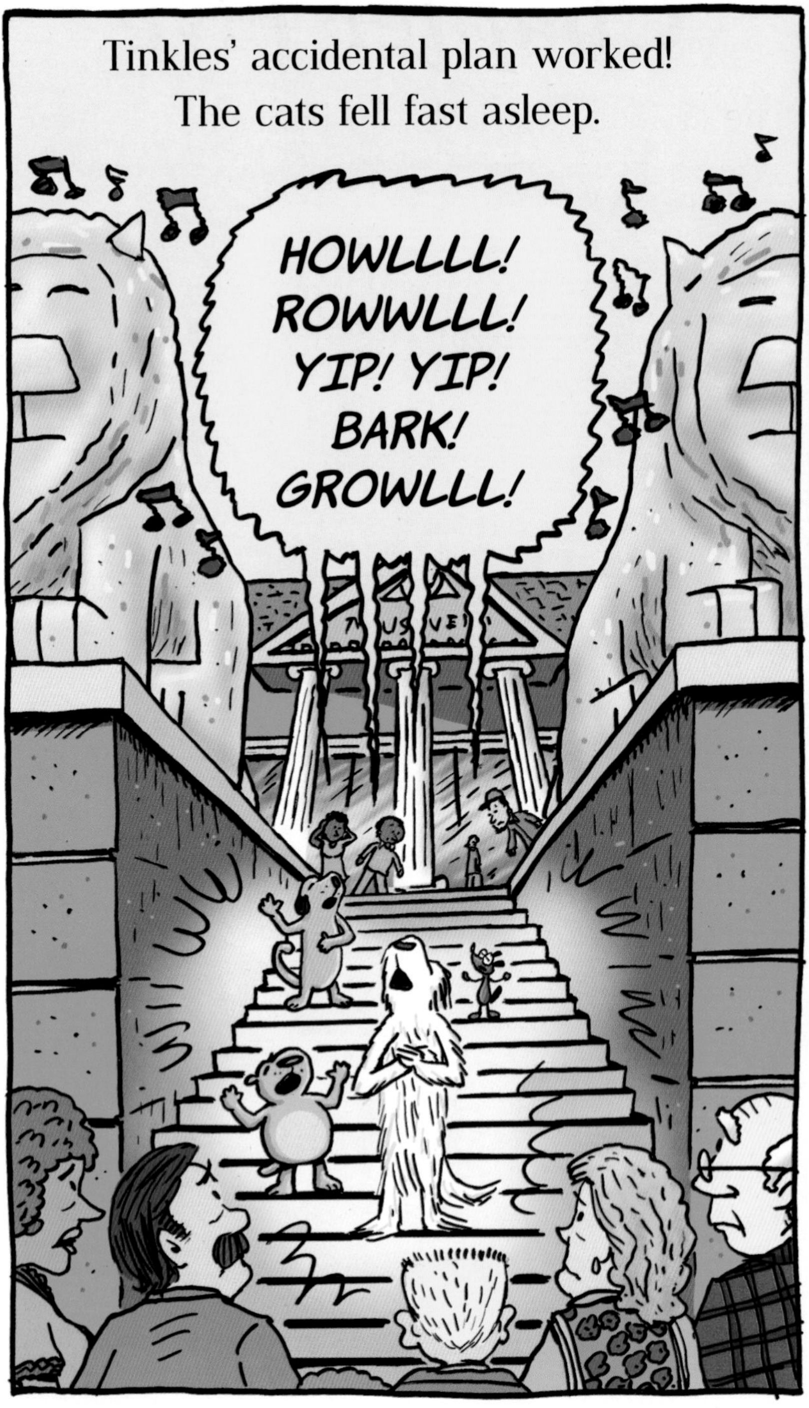
Tinkles' accidental plan worked!
The cats fell fast asleep.
HOWLLLL! ROWWLLL! YIP! YIP! BARK! GROWLLL!

Chapter Five

The crew of the HMS Minivan had arrived.

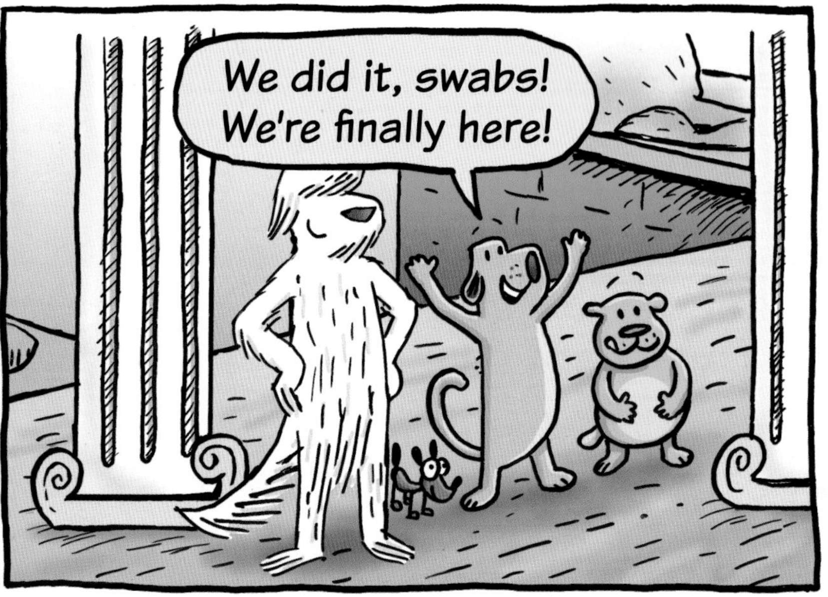
We did it, swabs!
We're finally here!

But nothing is ever easy for the Scurvy Dogs.

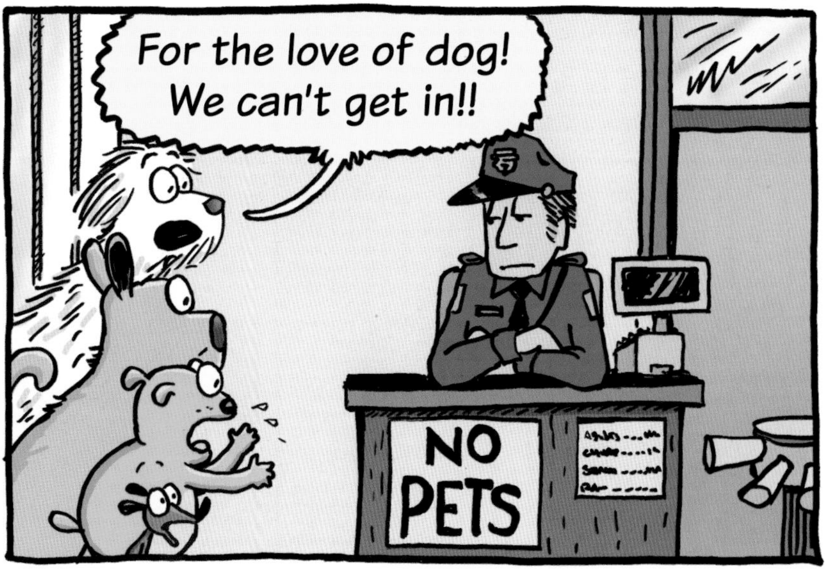
For the love of dog!
We can't get in!!
NO PETS

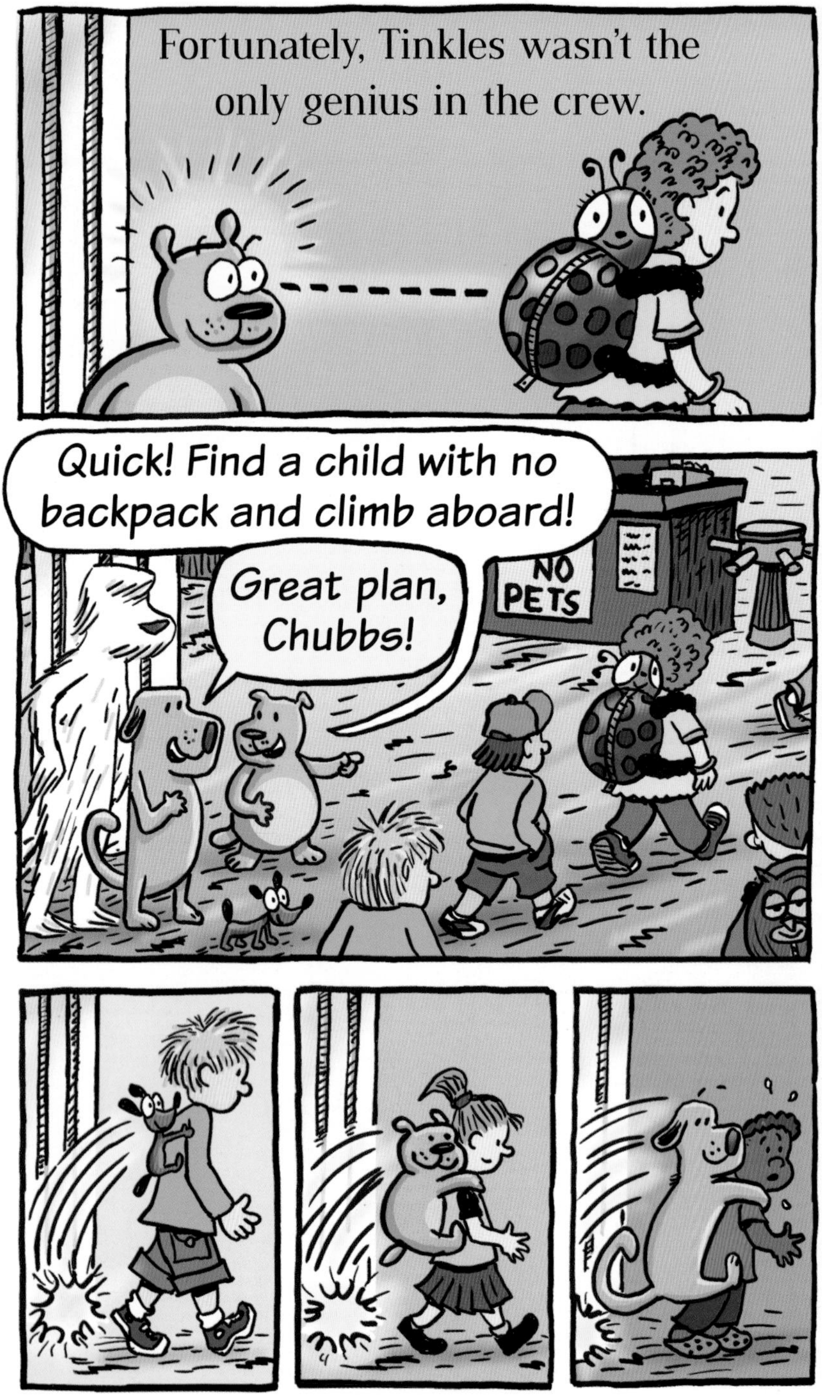

Fortunately, Tinkles wasn't the only genius in the crew.
Quick! Find a child with no backpack and climb aboard!
Great plan, Chubbs!
NO PETS

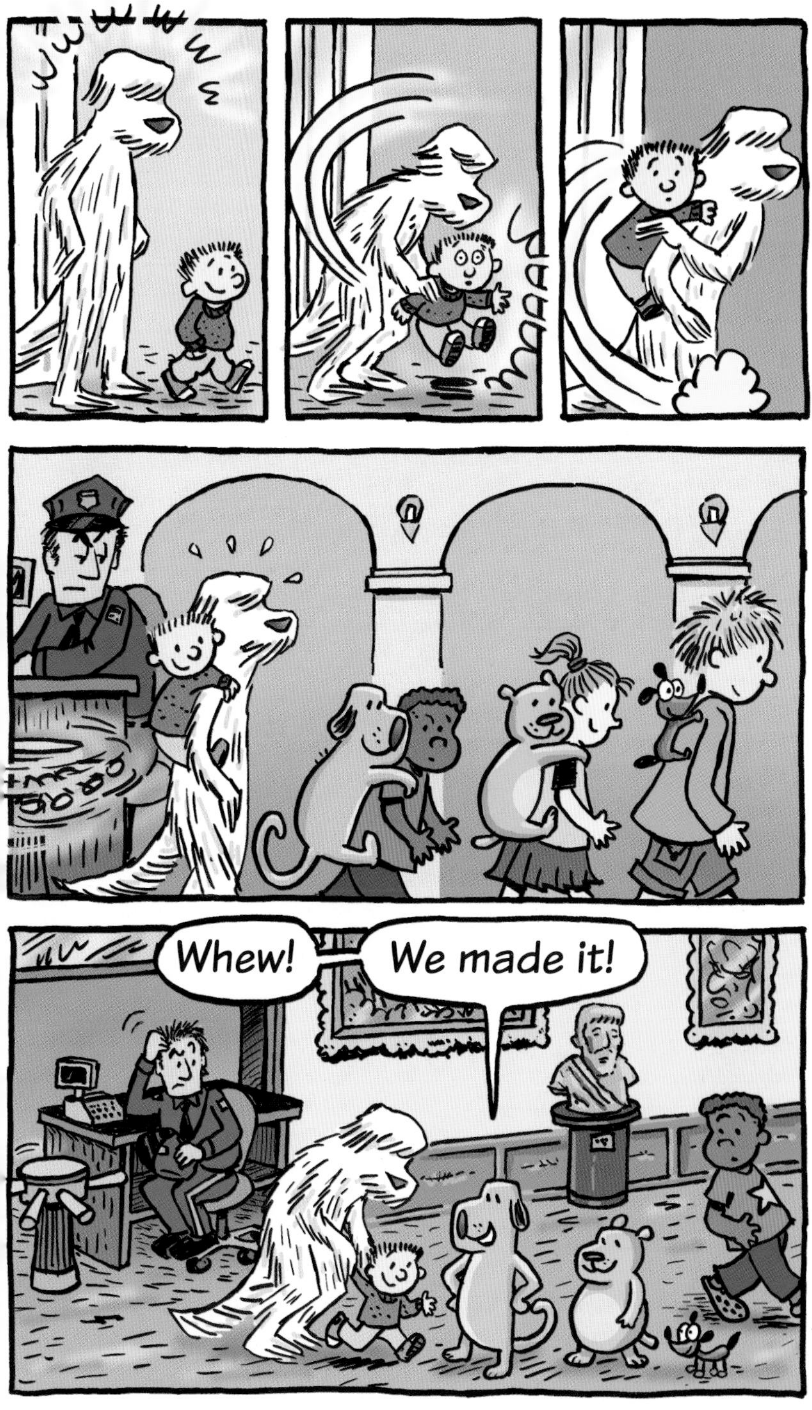
Whew!
We made it!

The hungry pirates were finally inside the Dinosaur Boneyard!

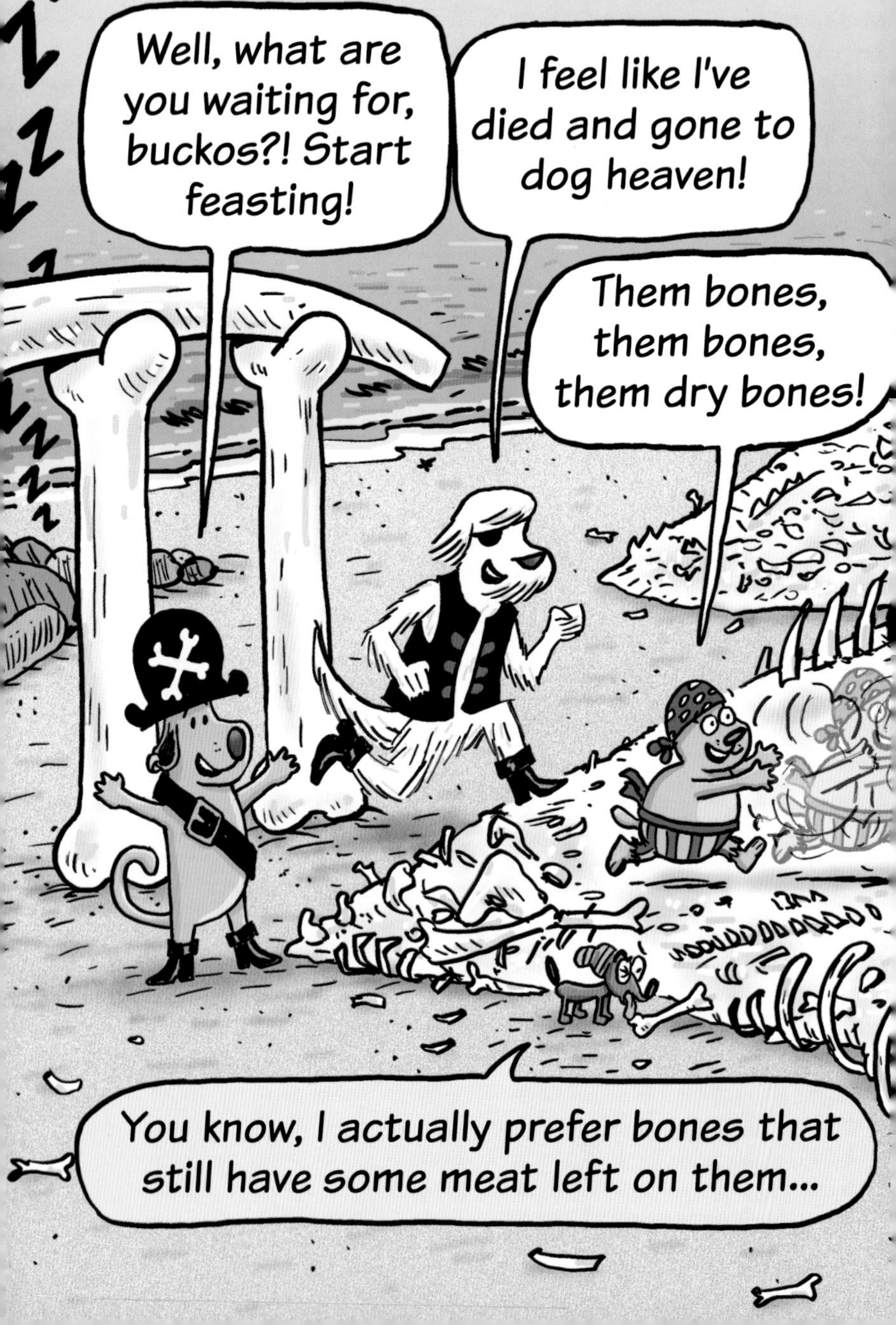
Well, what are you waiting for, buckos?! Start feasting!
I feel like I've died and gone to dog heaven!
Them bones, them bones, them dry bones!
You know, I actually prefer bones that still have some meat left on them...

But then… you guessed it!

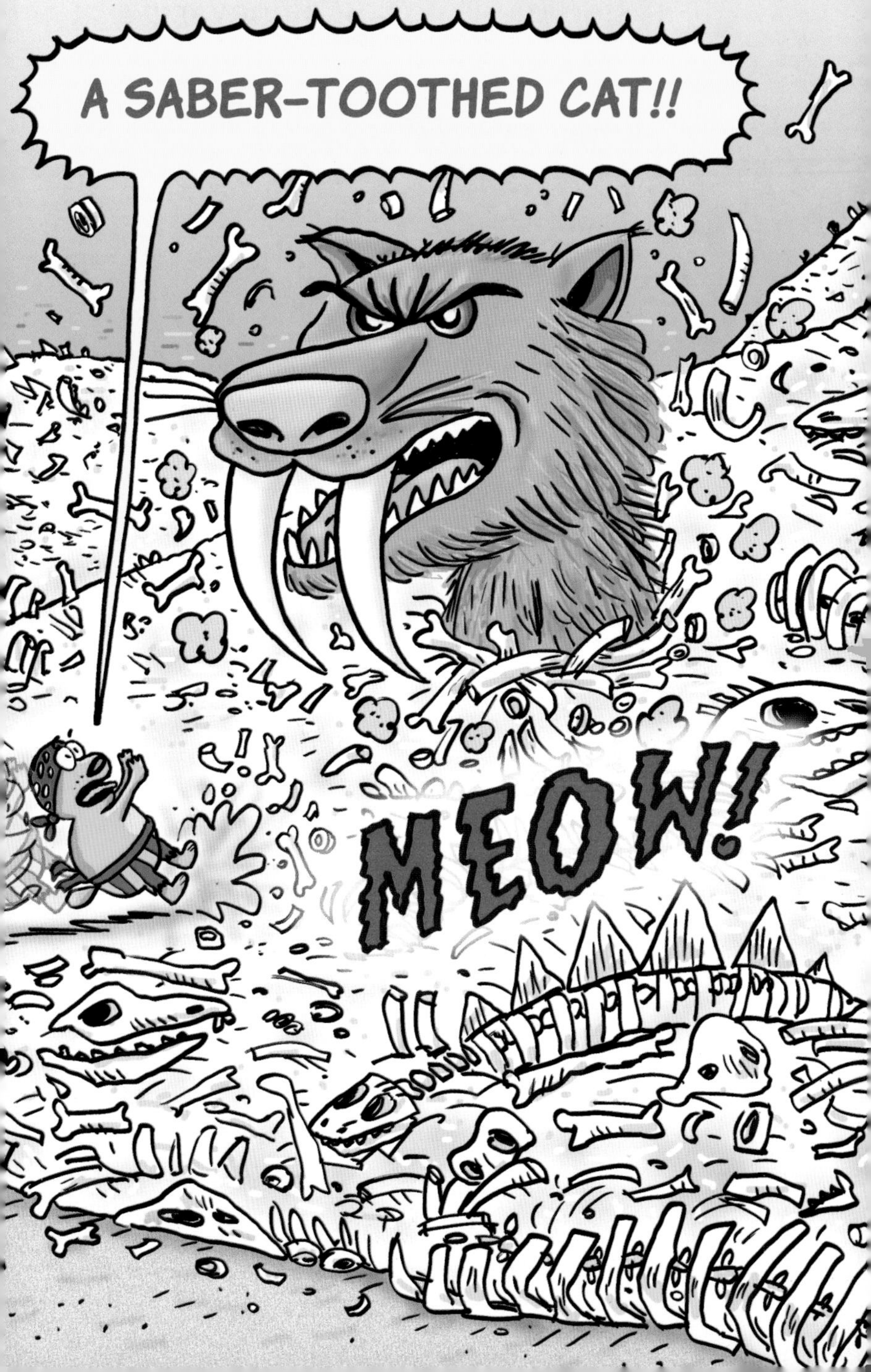

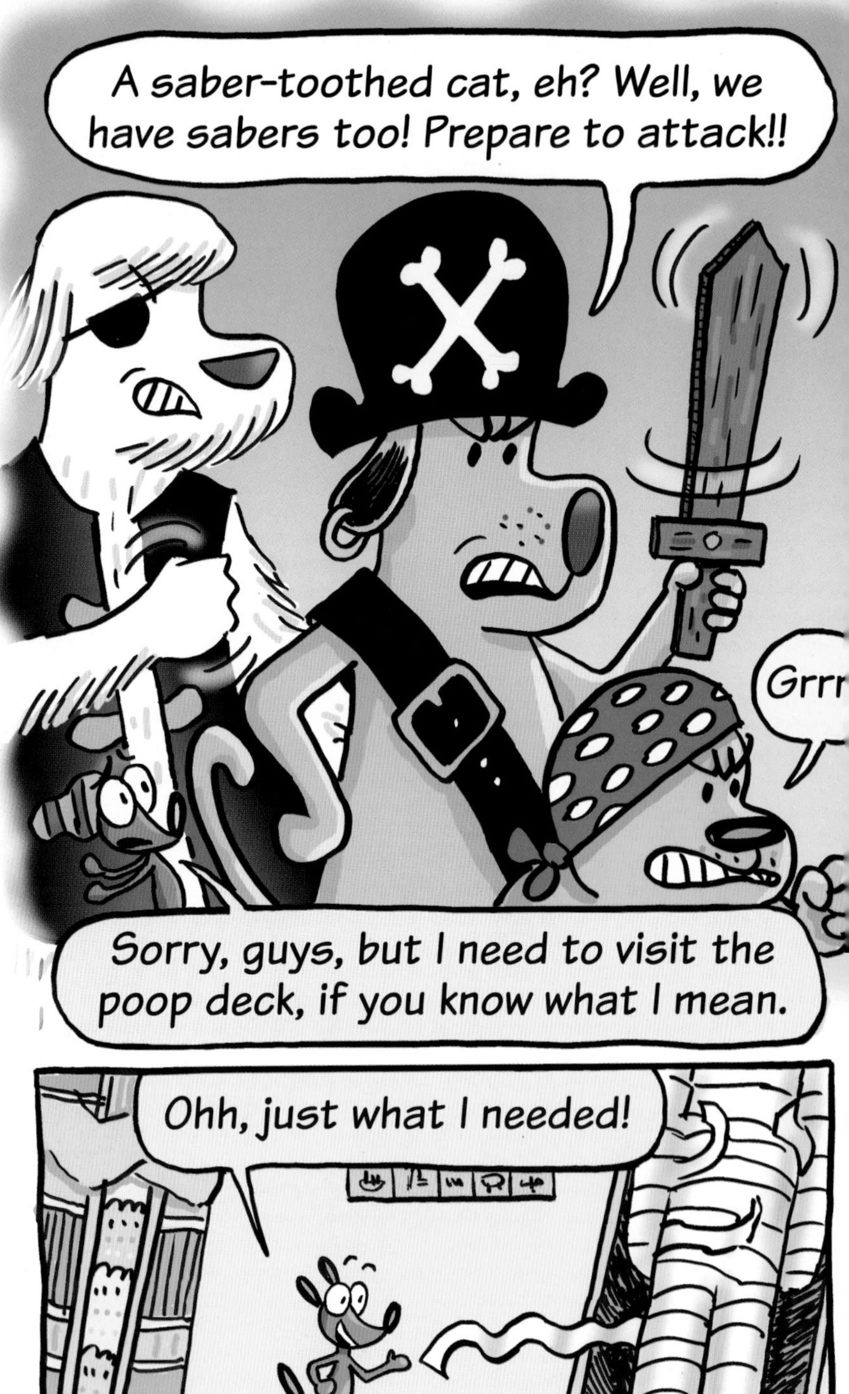
A saber-toothed cat, eh? Well, we have sabers too! Prepare to attack!!
Grrr
Sorry, guys, but I need to visit the poop deck, if you know what I mean.
Ohh, just what I needed!

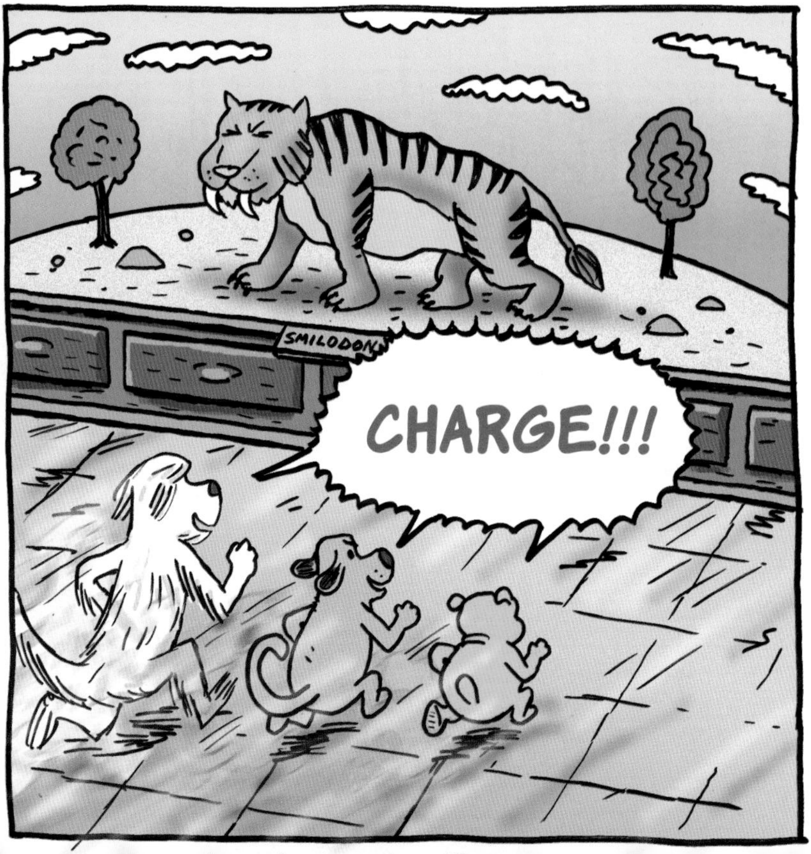
SMILODON
CHARGE!!!

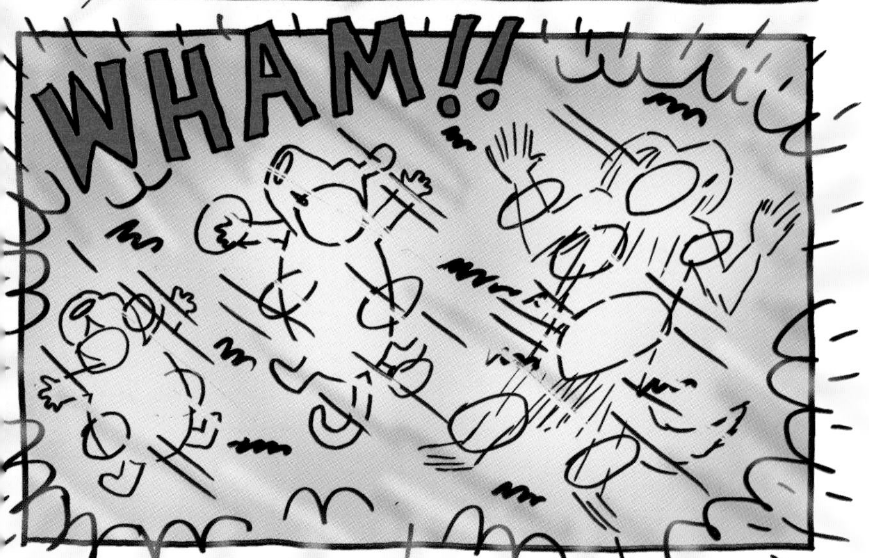
WHAM!!

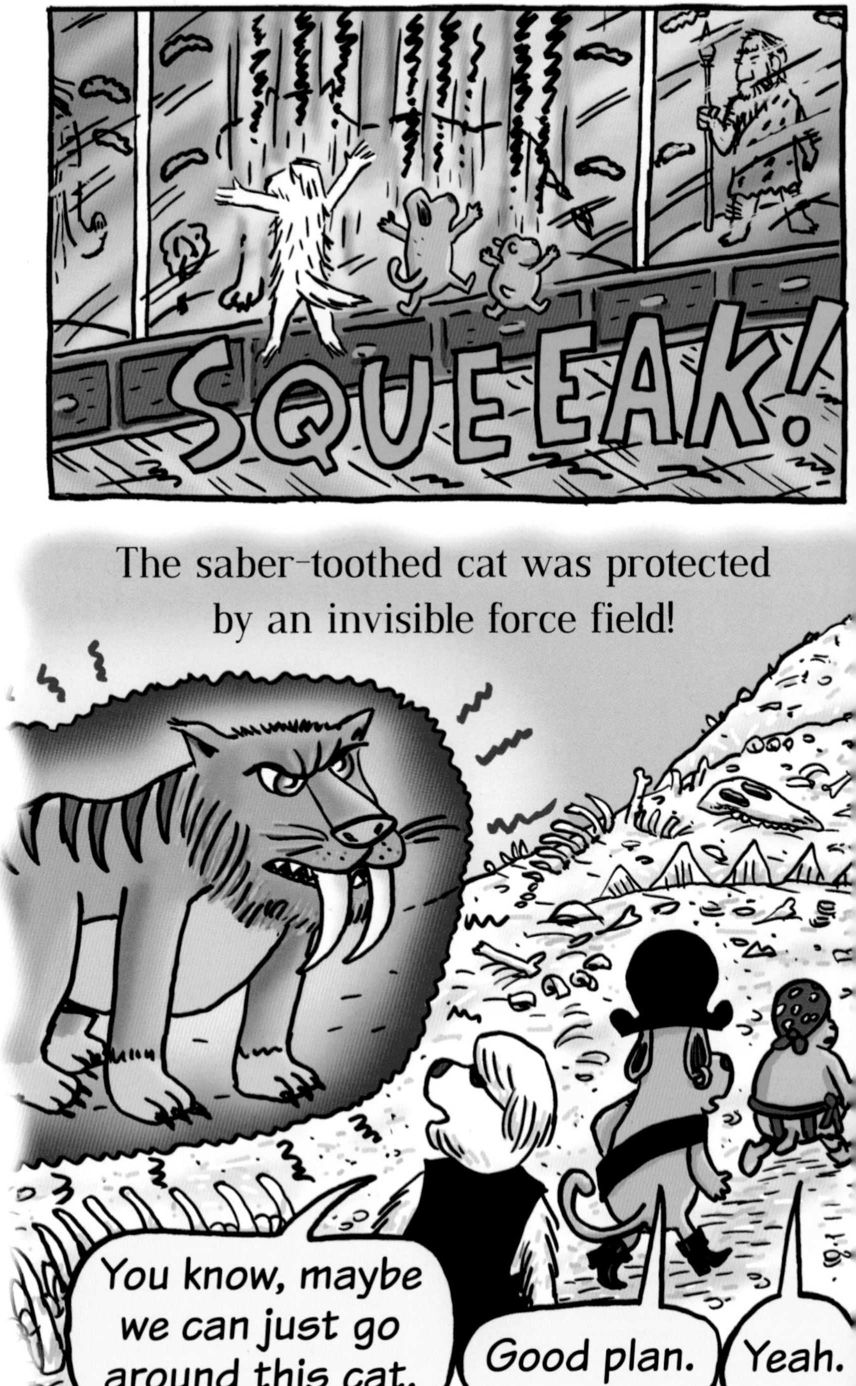
SQUEEAK!
The saber-toothed cat was protected by an invisible force field!
You know, maybe we can just go around this cat.
Good plan.
Yeah.

Chapter Six

The defeated dogs walked away, licking their wounds.

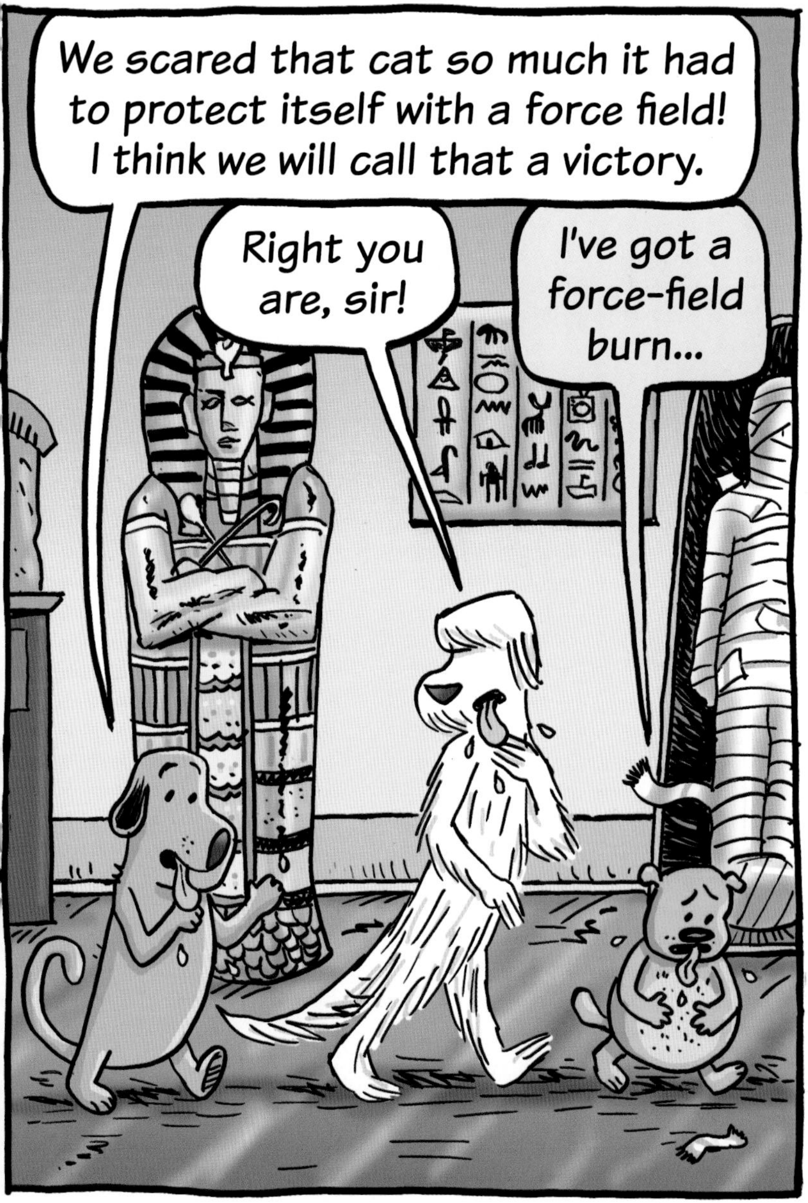
We scared that cat so much it had to protect itself with a force field! I think we will call that a victory.
Right you are, sir!
I've got a force-field burn...

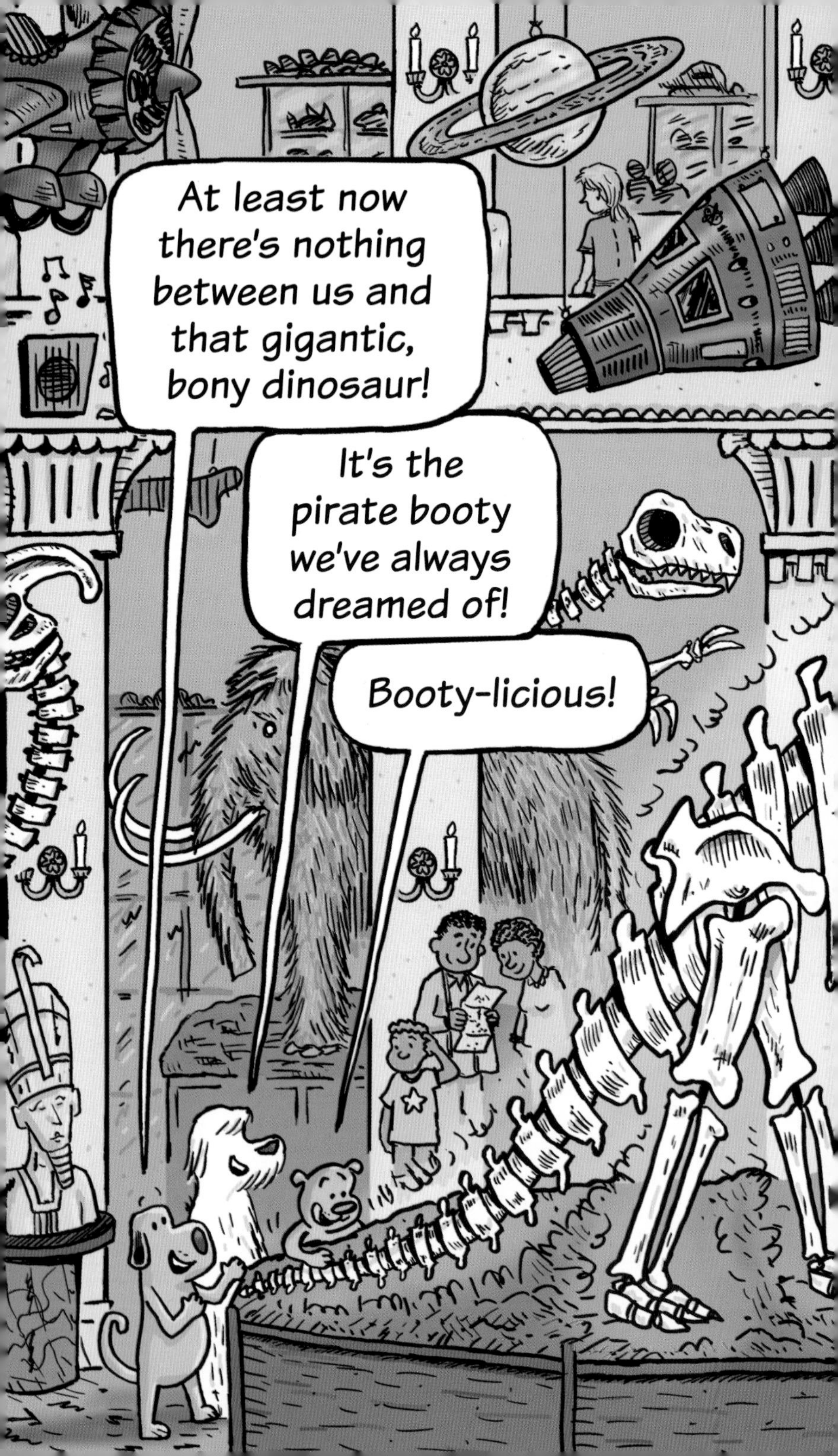
At least now there's nothing between us and that gigantic, bony dinosaur!
It's the pirate booty we've always dreamed of!
Booty-licious!

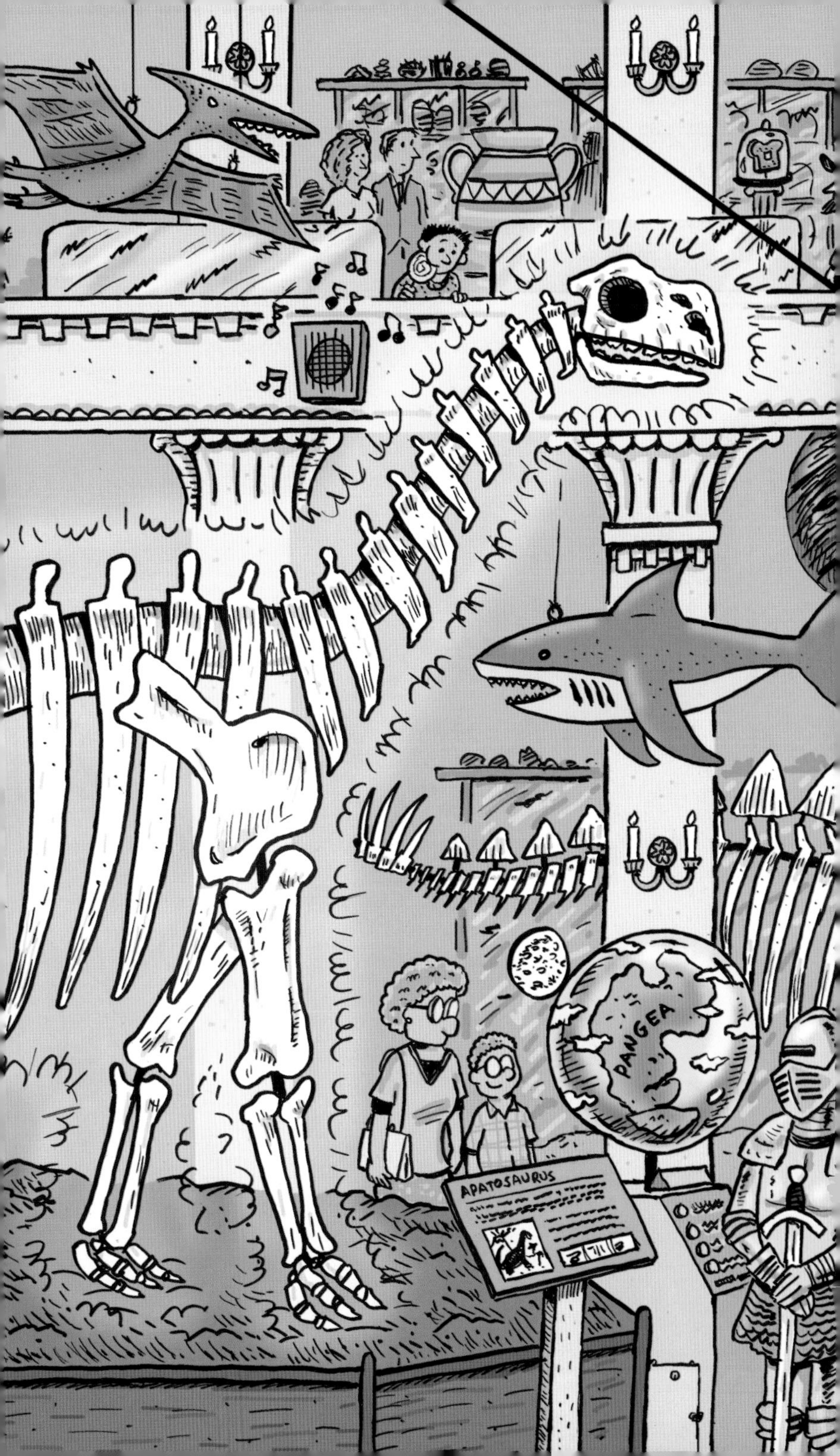
PANGEA
APATOSAURUS

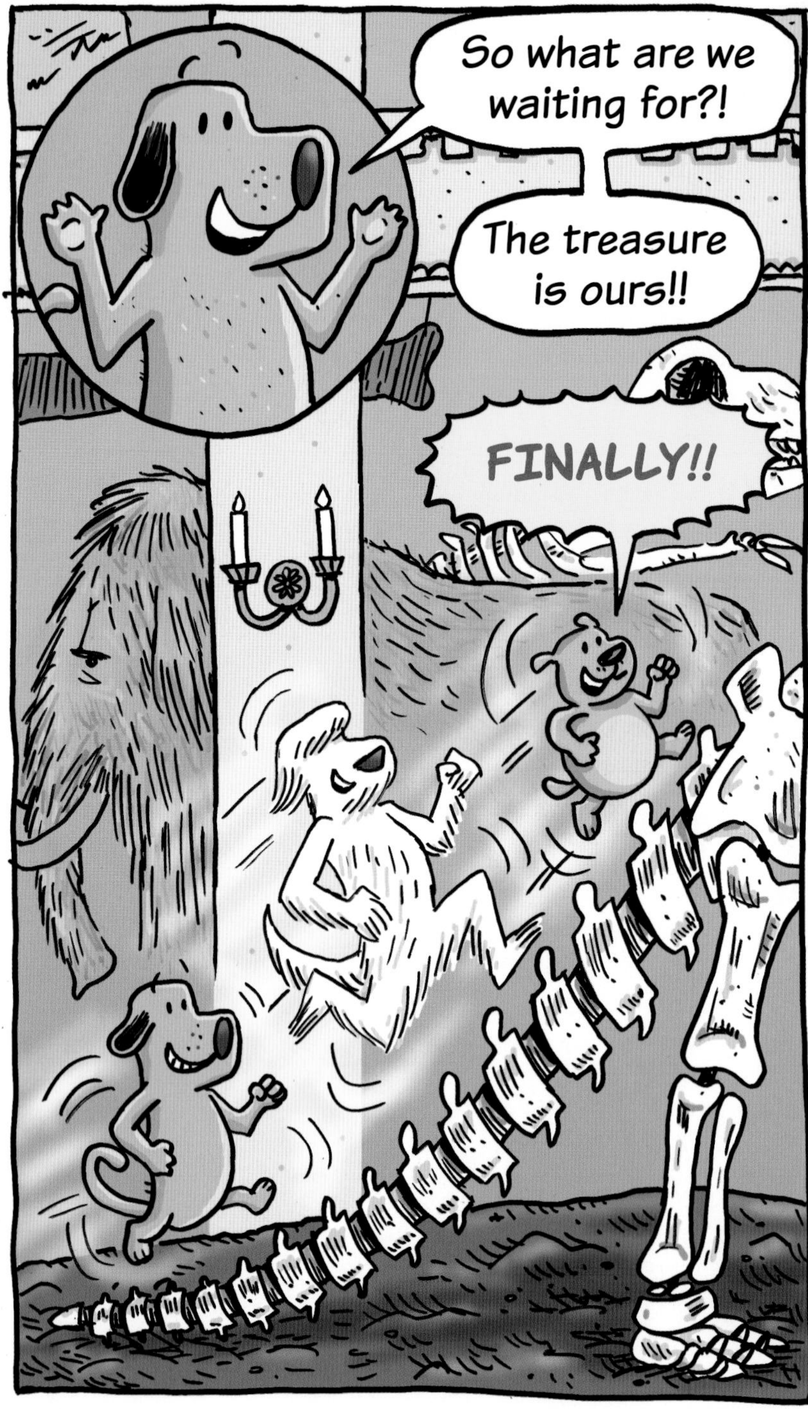
So what are we waiting for?!
The treasure is ours!!
FINALLY!!

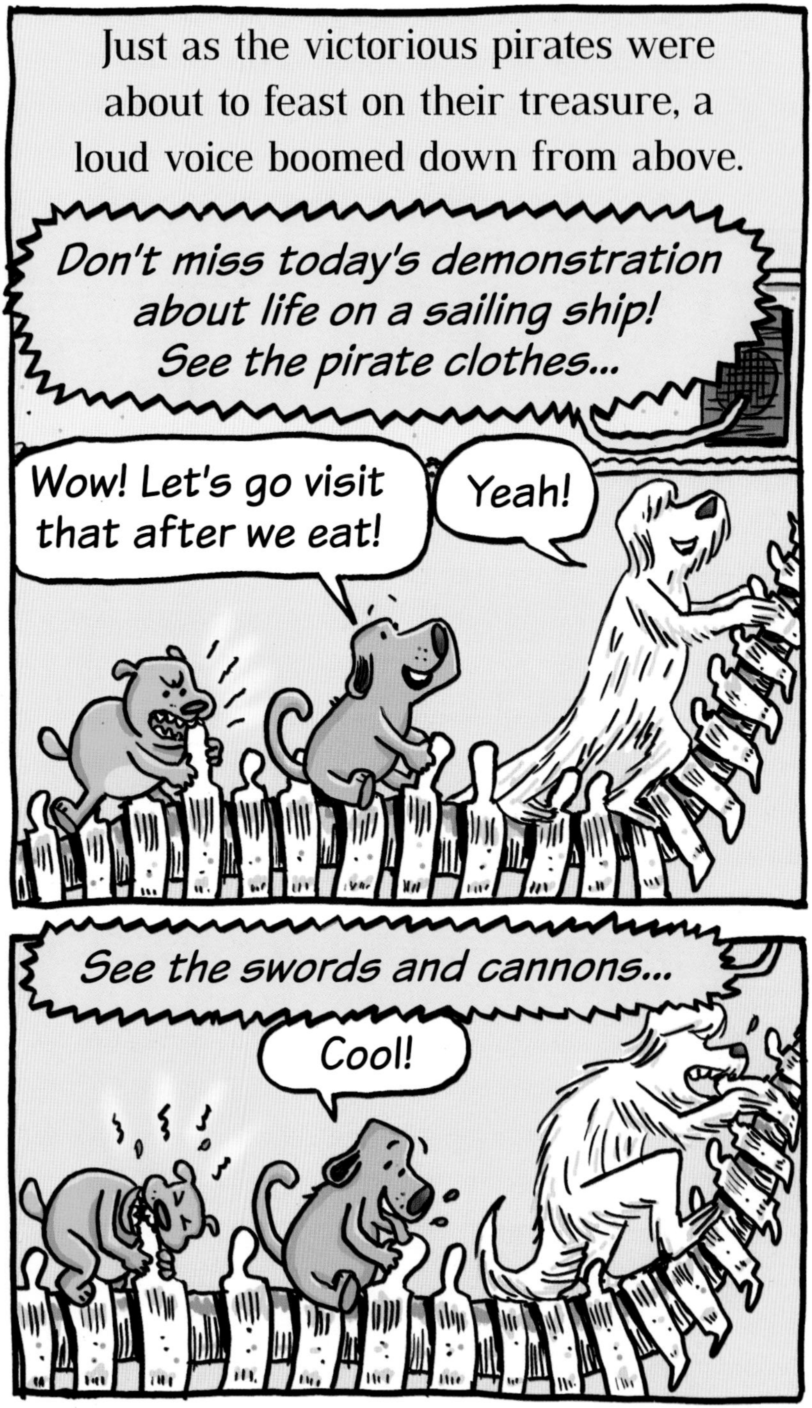
Just as the victorious pirates were about to feast on their treasure, a loud voice boomed down from above.
Don't miss today's demonstration about life on a sailing ship! See the pirate clothes...
Wow! Let's go visit that after we eat!
Yeah!
See the swords and cannons...
Cool!

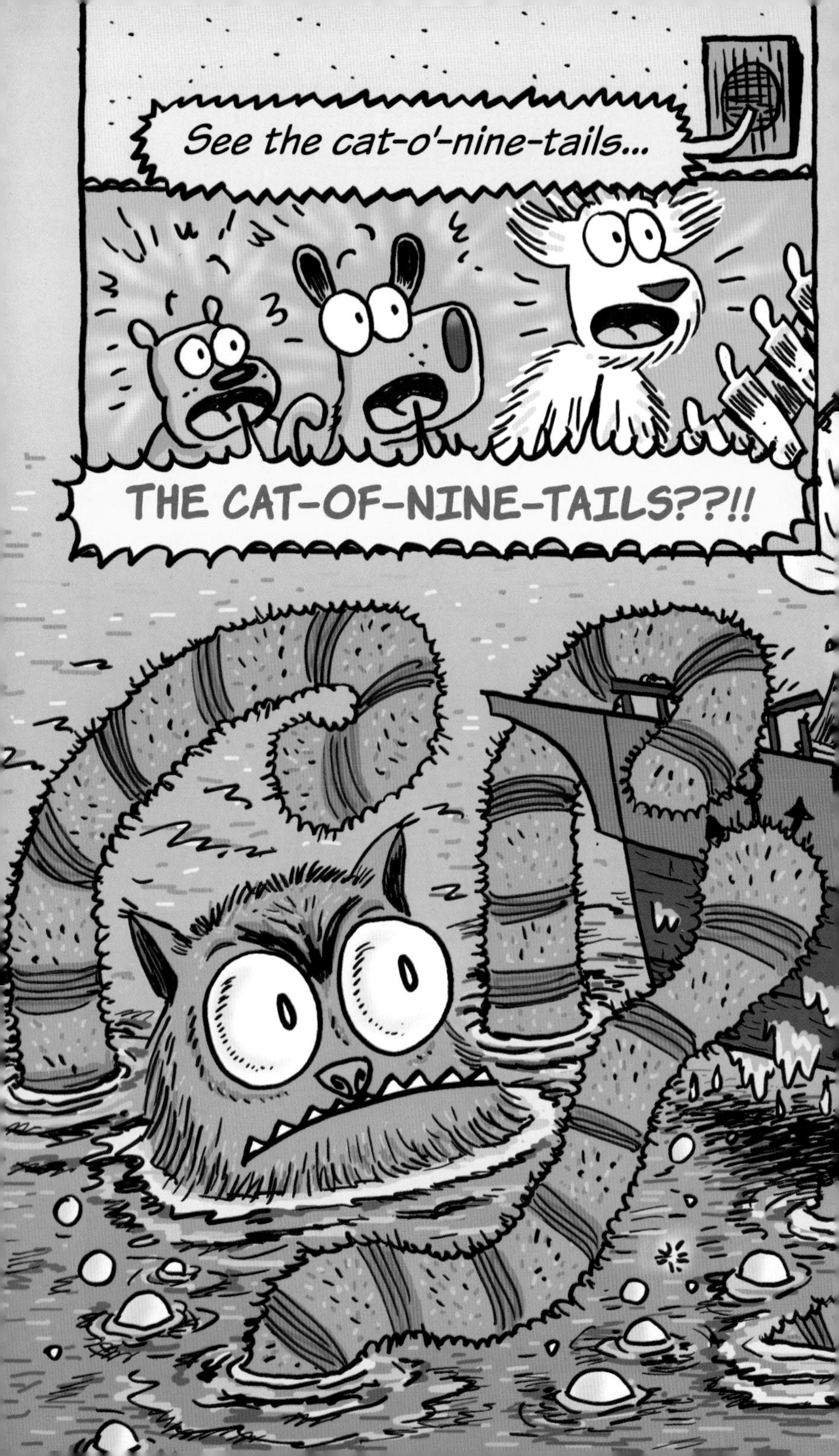
See the cat-o'-nine-tails...
THE CAT-OF-NINE-TAILS??!!

The Cat-Of-Nine-Tails was a legendary sea monster. It would rise from the depths of the ocean to crush a ship within the coils of its nine massive tails. The horrible creature was a sailor's worst nightmare. And it was HERE!

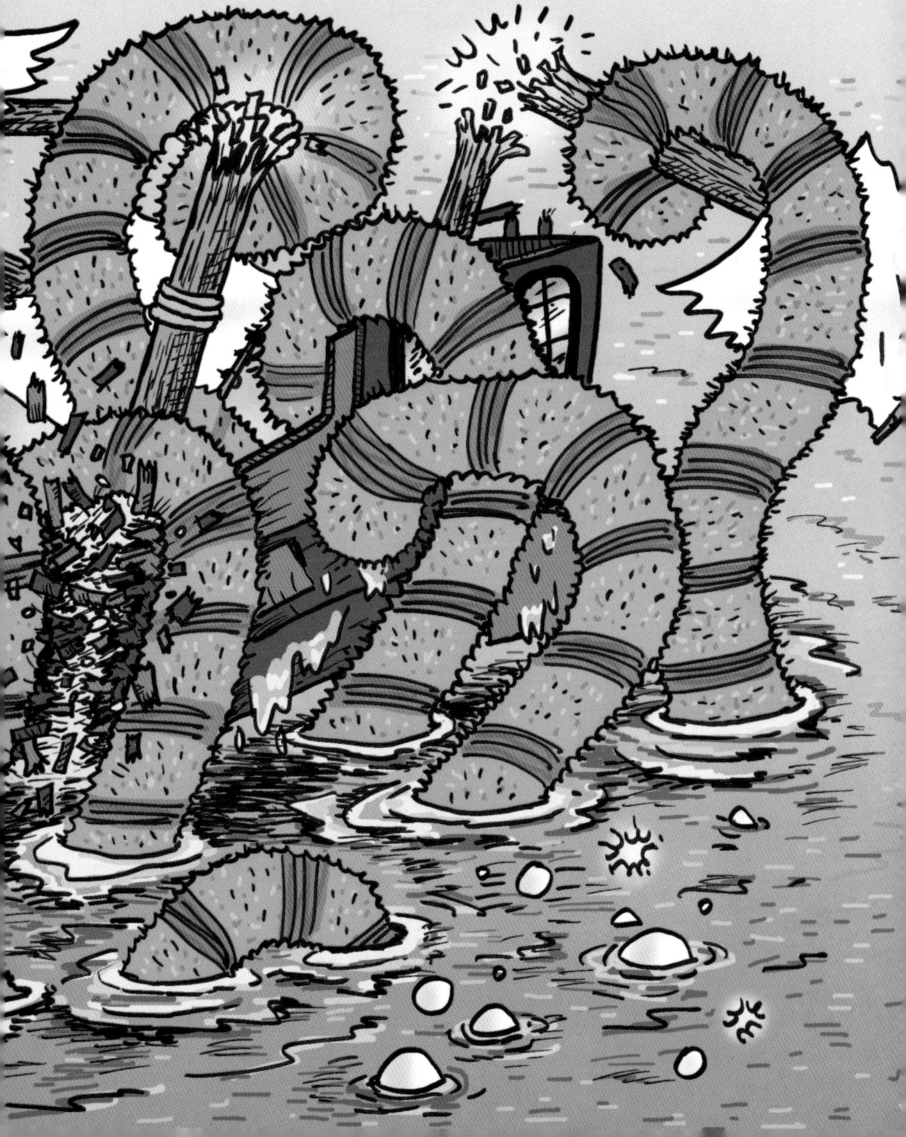

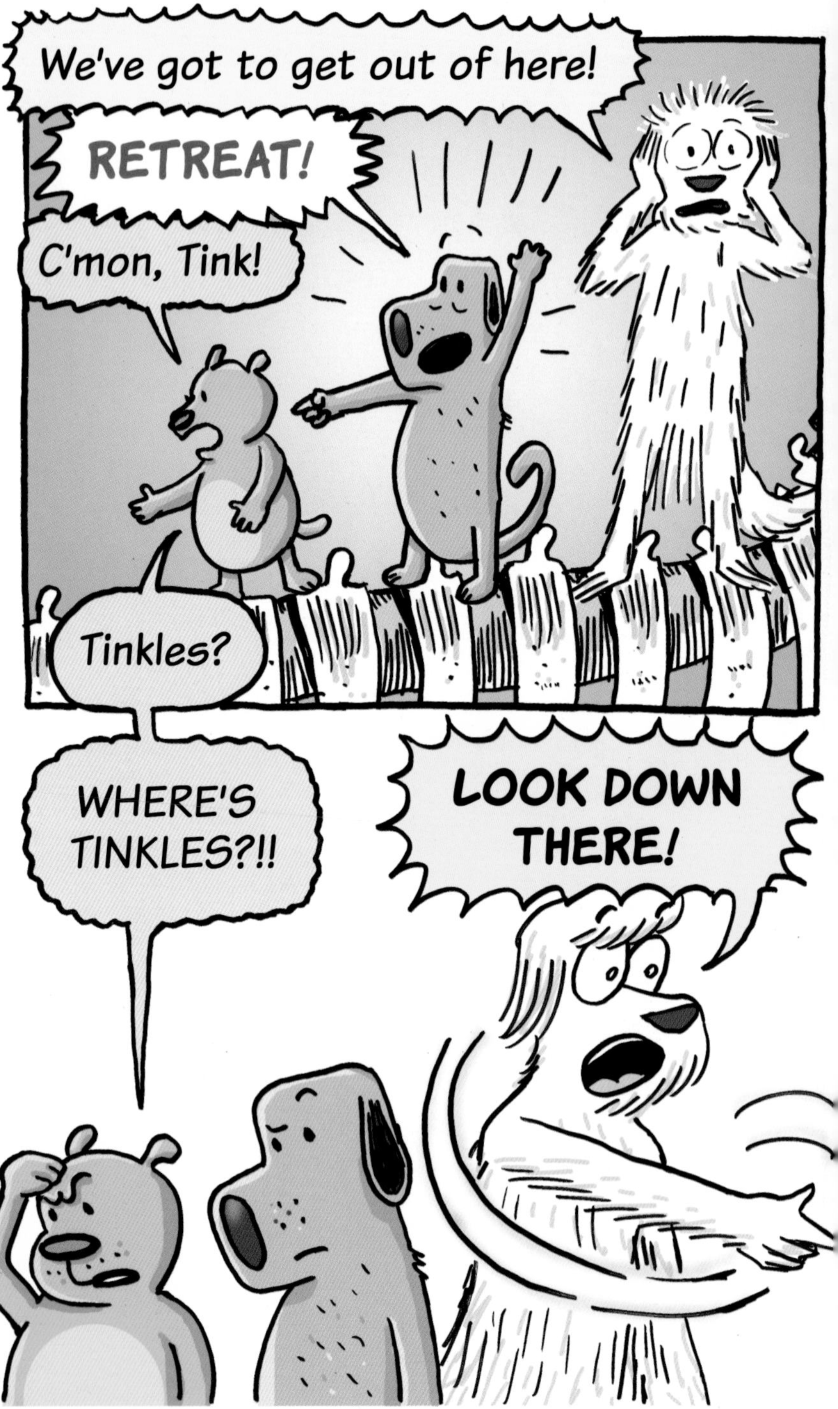
We've got to get out of here!
RETREAT!
C'mon, Tink!
Tinkles?
WHERE'S TINKLES?!!
LOOK DOWN THERE!

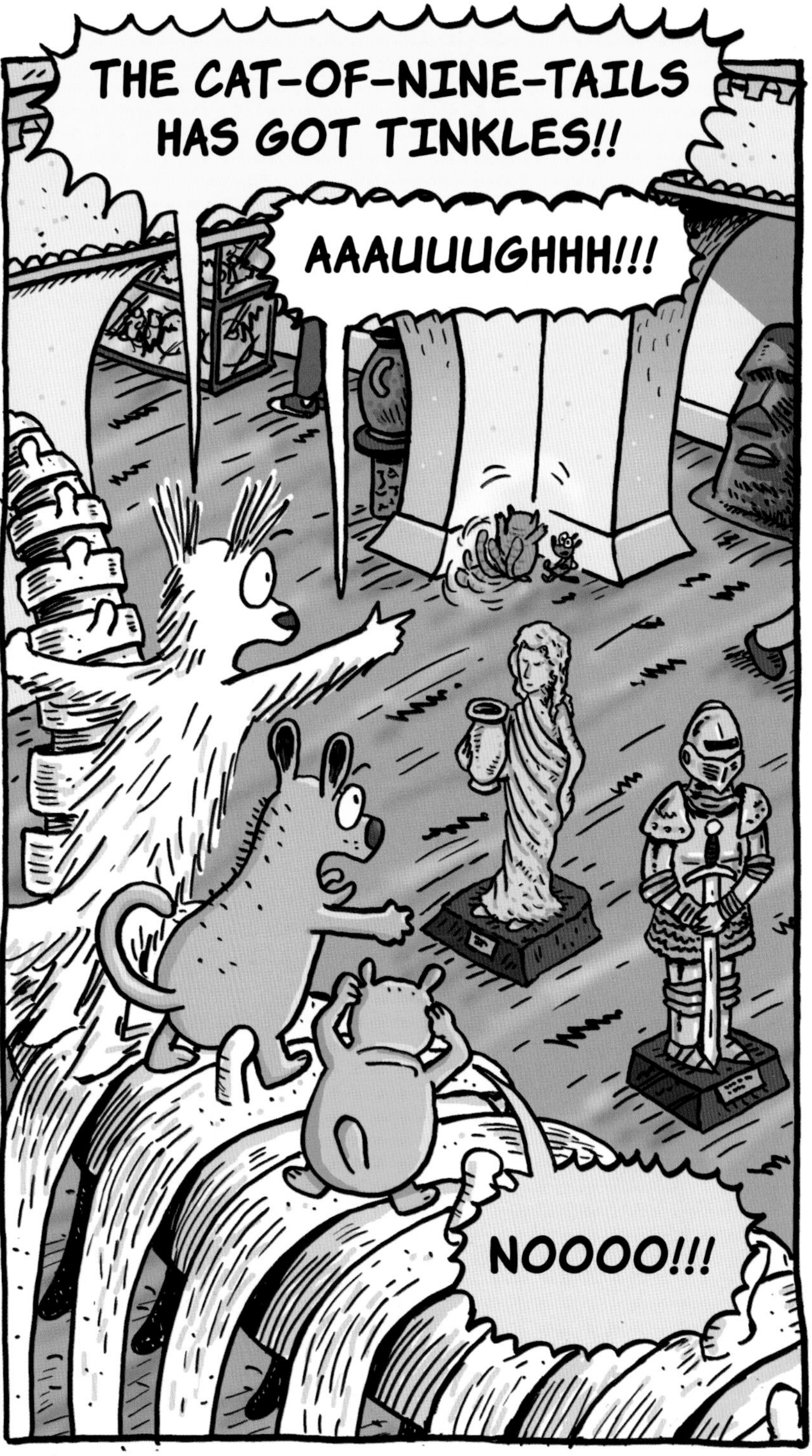
THE CAT-OF-NINE-TAILS HAS GOT TINKLES!!
AAAUUUGHHH!!!
NOOOO!!!

Chapter Seven

The hideous, disgusting Cat-of-Nine-Tails had captured Tinkles.

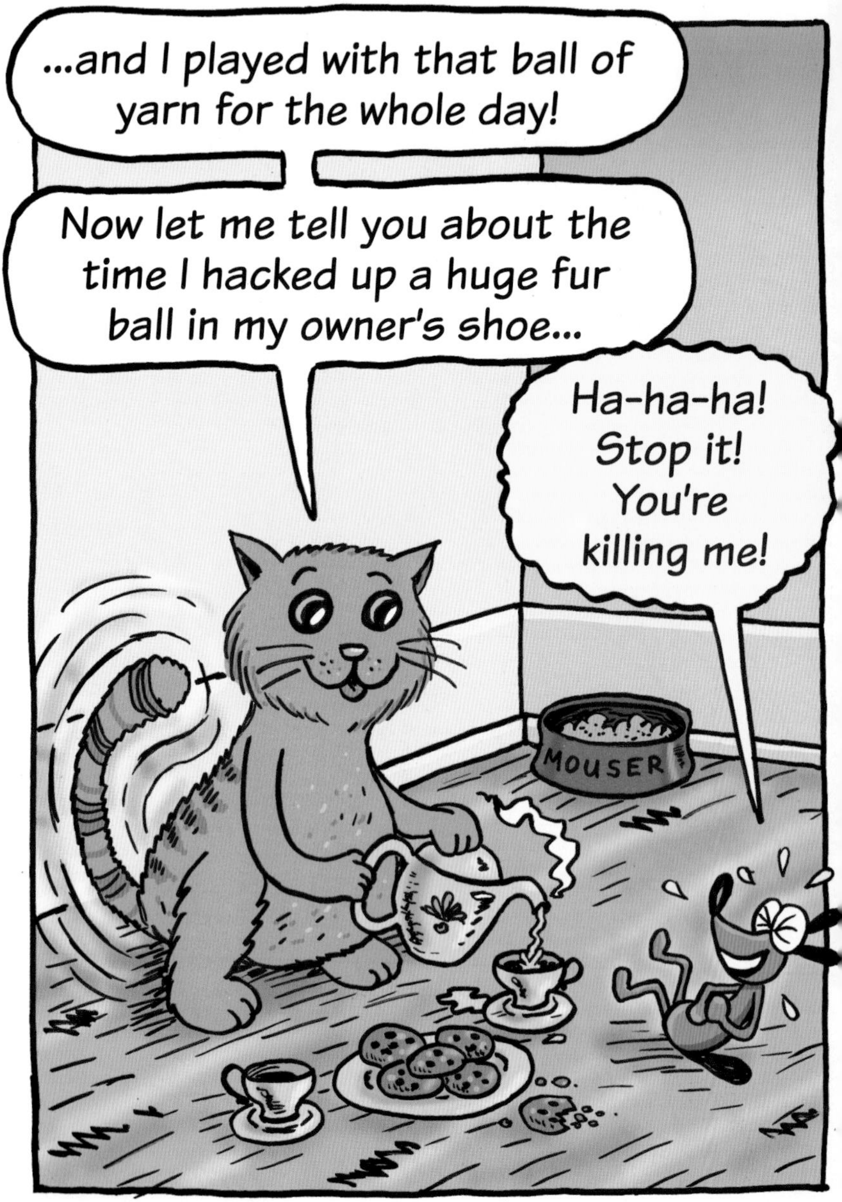

...and I played with that ball of yarn for the whole day!
Now let me tell you about the time I hacked up a huge fur ball in my owner's shoe...
Ha-ha-ha! Stop it! You're killing me!
MOUSER

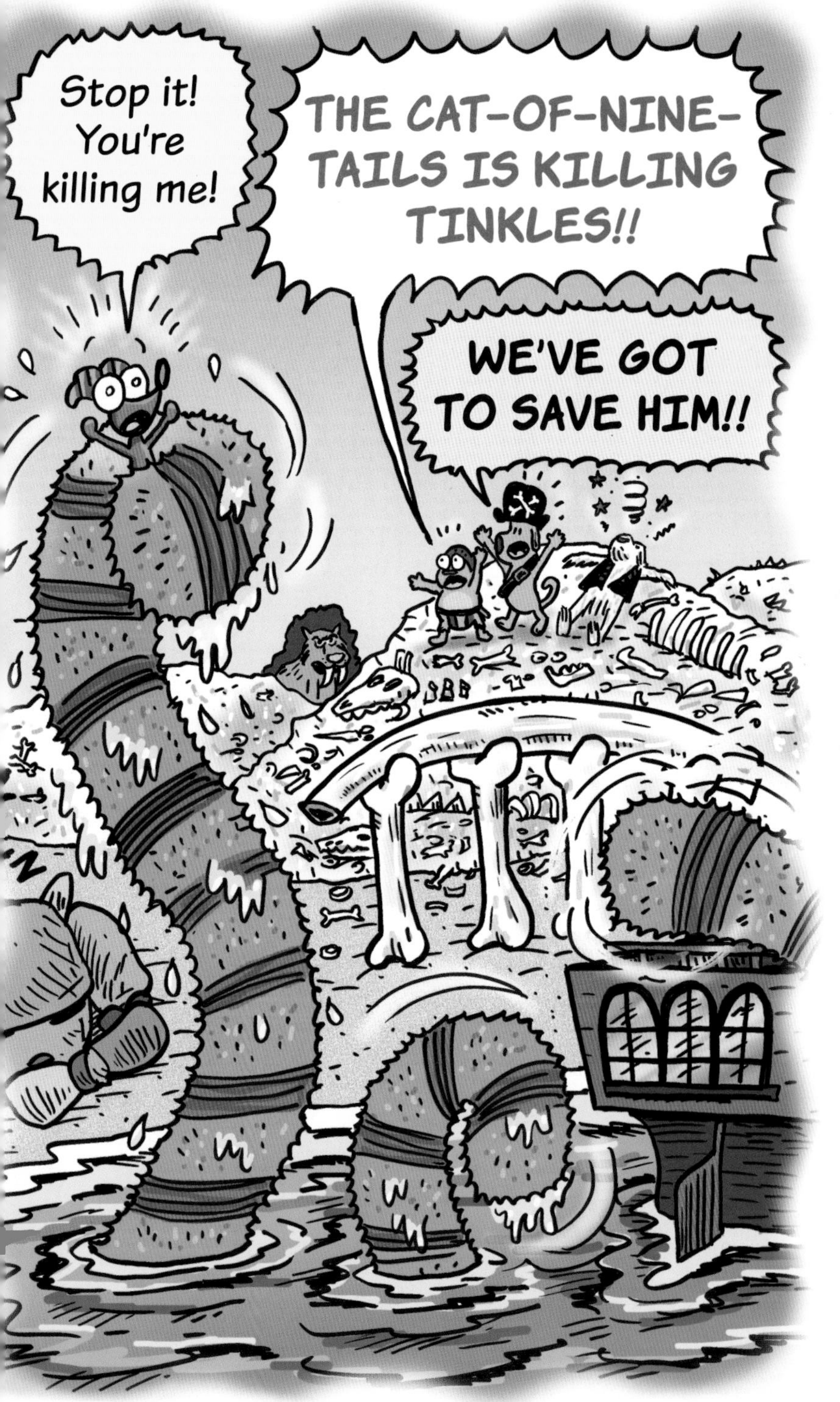
Stop it! You're killing me!
THE CAT-OF-NINE-TAILS IS KILLING TINKLES!!
WE'VE GOT TO SAVE HIM!!

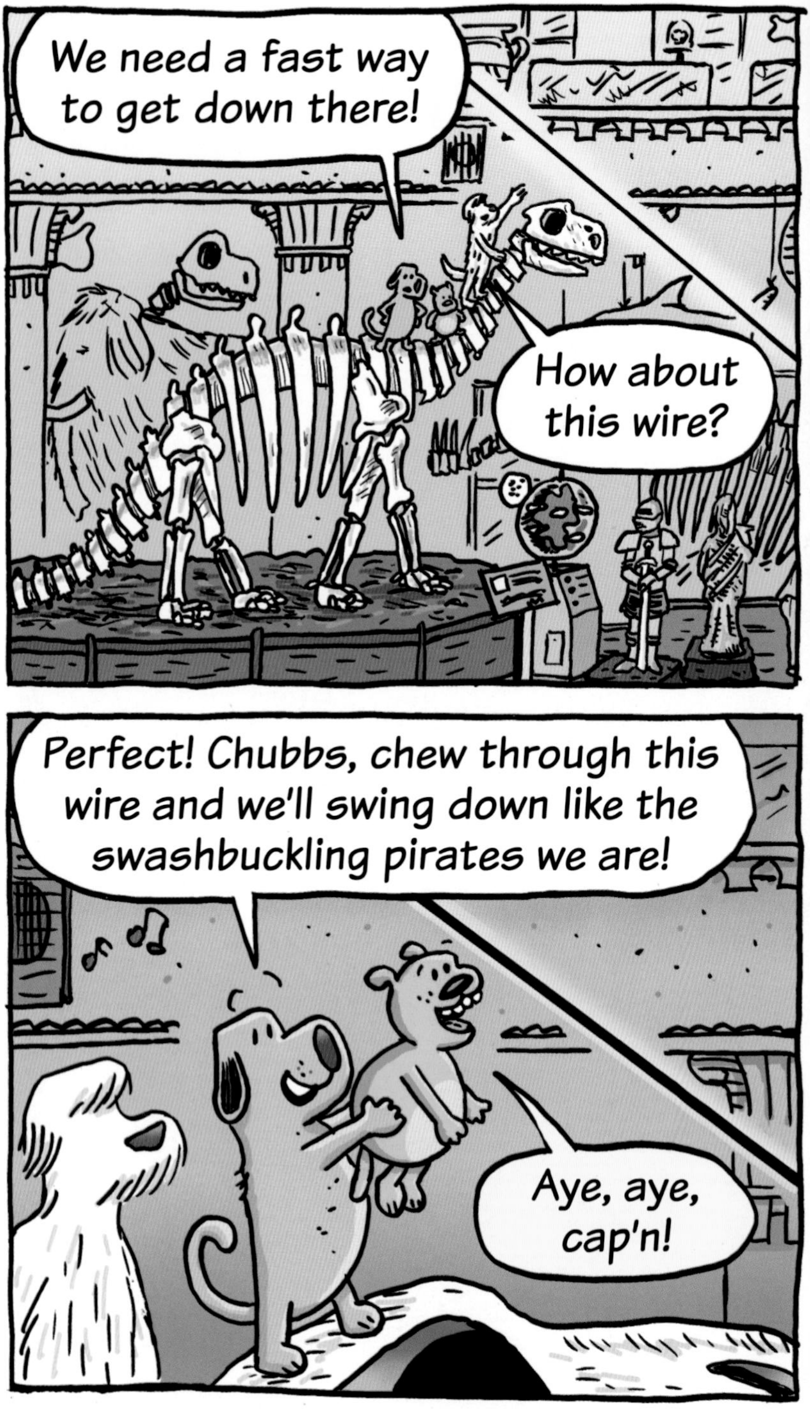
We need a fast way to get down there!
How about this wire?
Perfect! Chubbs, chew through this wire and we'll swing down like the swashbuckling pirates we are!
Aye, aye, cap'n!

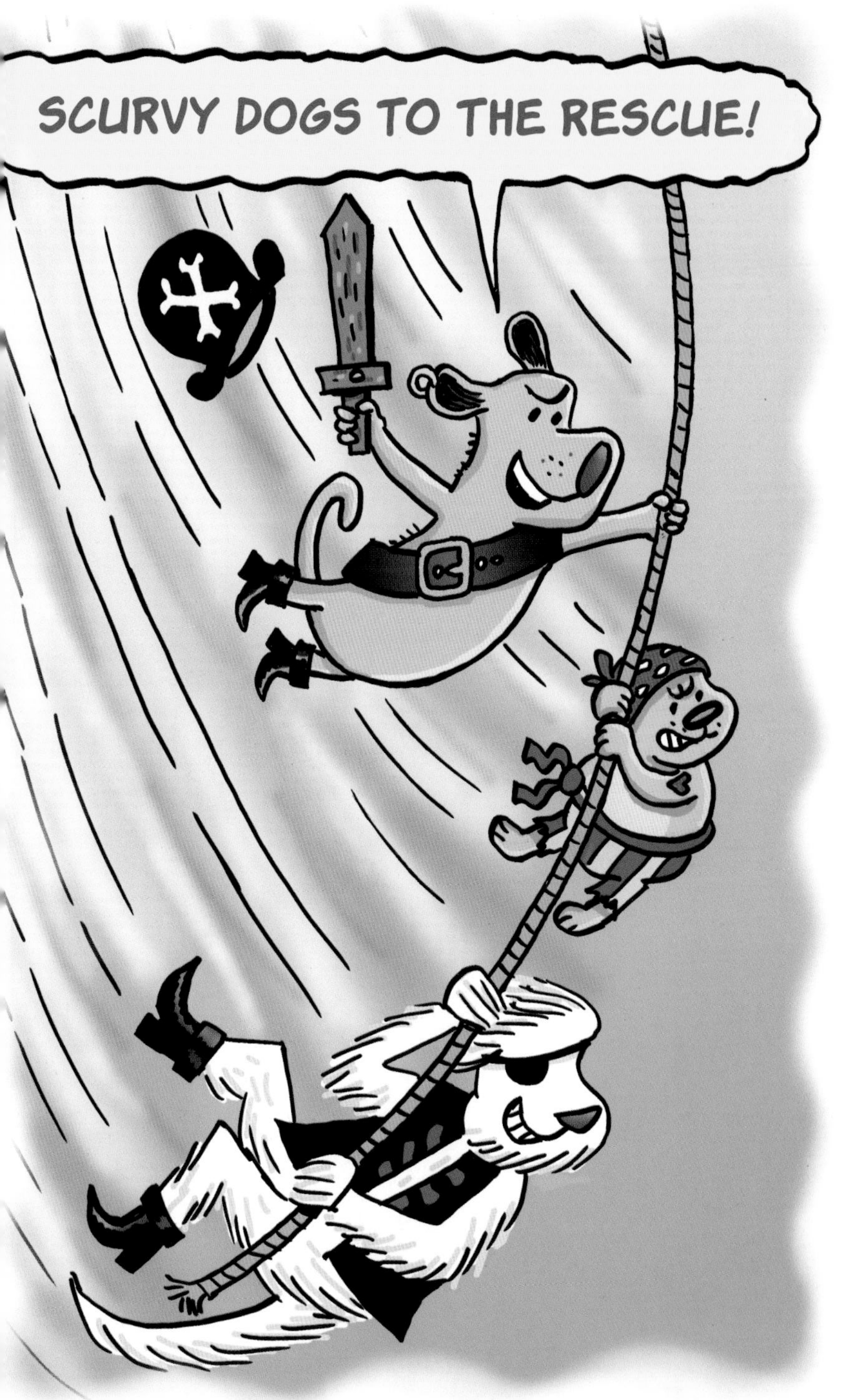
SCURVY DOGS TO THE RESCUE!

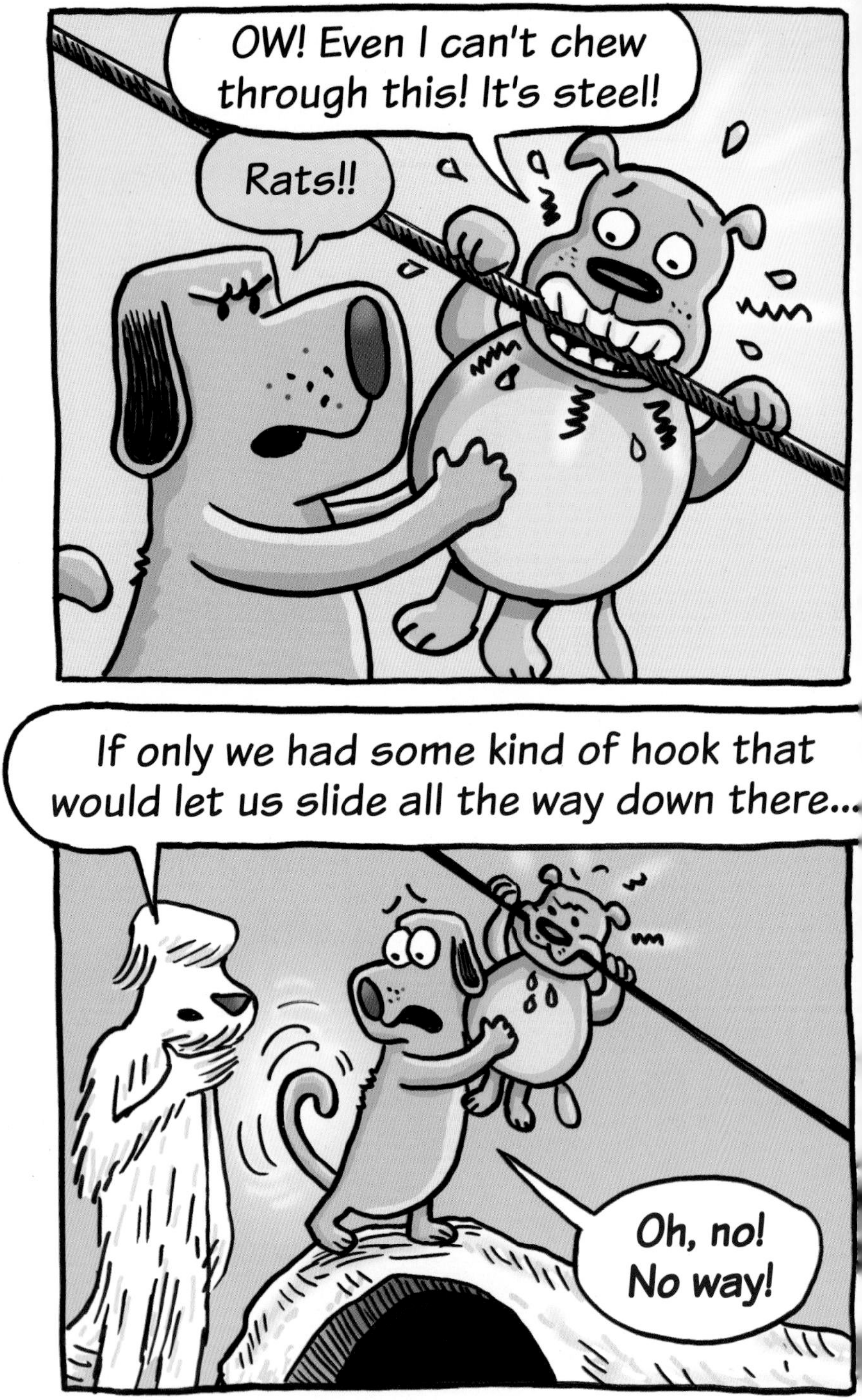

OW! Even I can't chew through this! It's steel!
Rats!!
If only we had some kind of hook that would let us slide all the way down there...
Oh, no! No way!

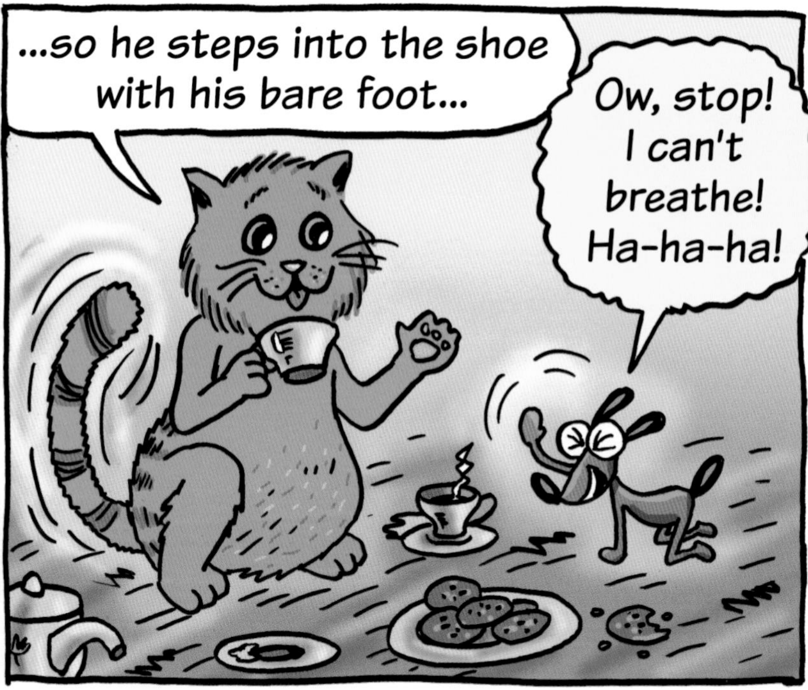
...so he steps into the shoe with his bare foot...
Ow, stop! I can't breathe! Ha-ha-ha!

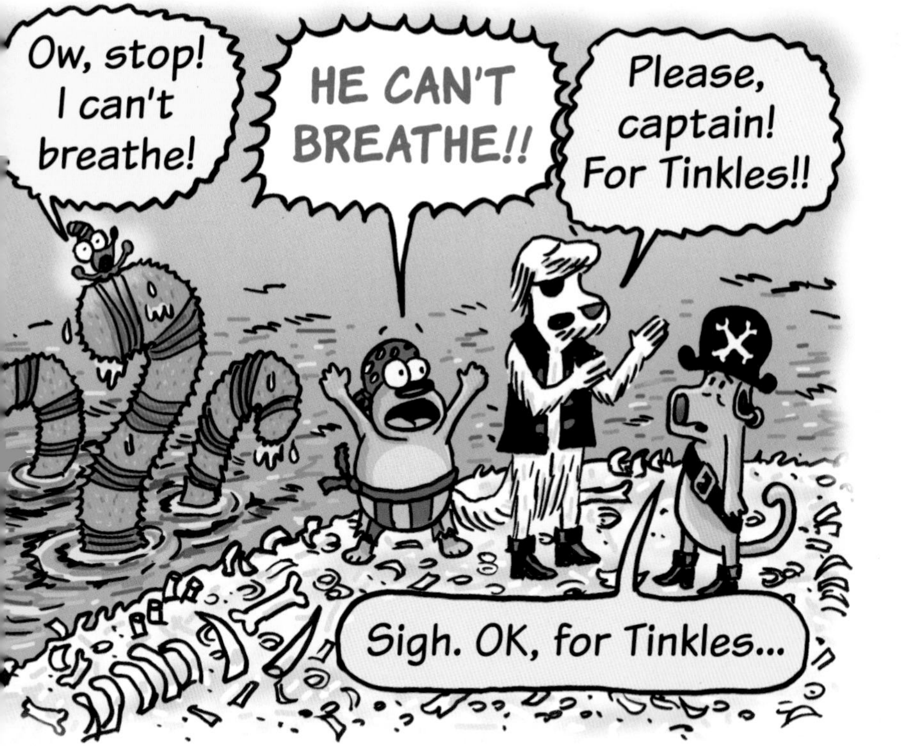
Ow, stop! I can't breathe!
HE CAN'T BREATHE!!
Please, captain! For Tinkles!!
Sigh. OK, for Tinkles...

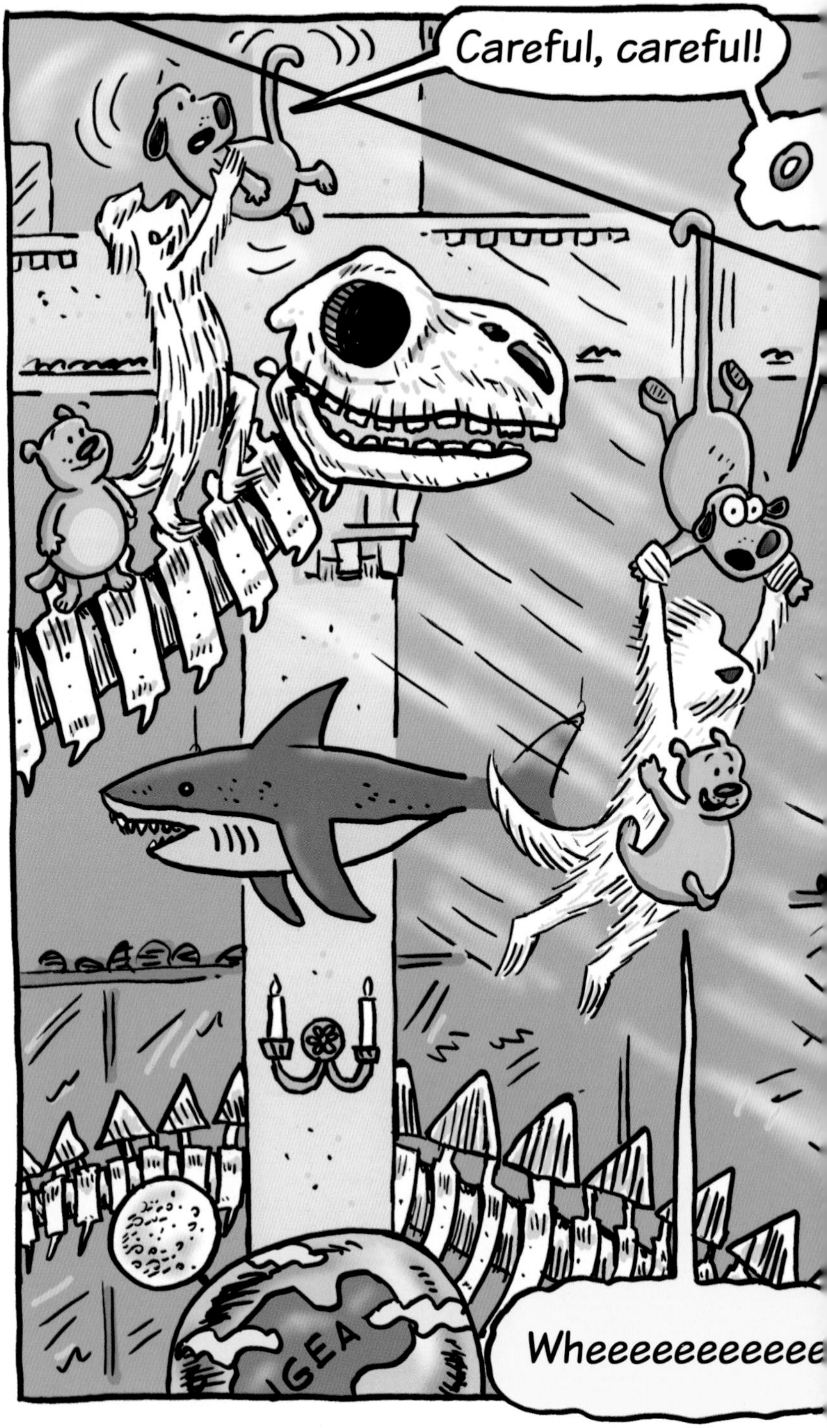
Careful, careful!
Wheeeeeeeeeeee

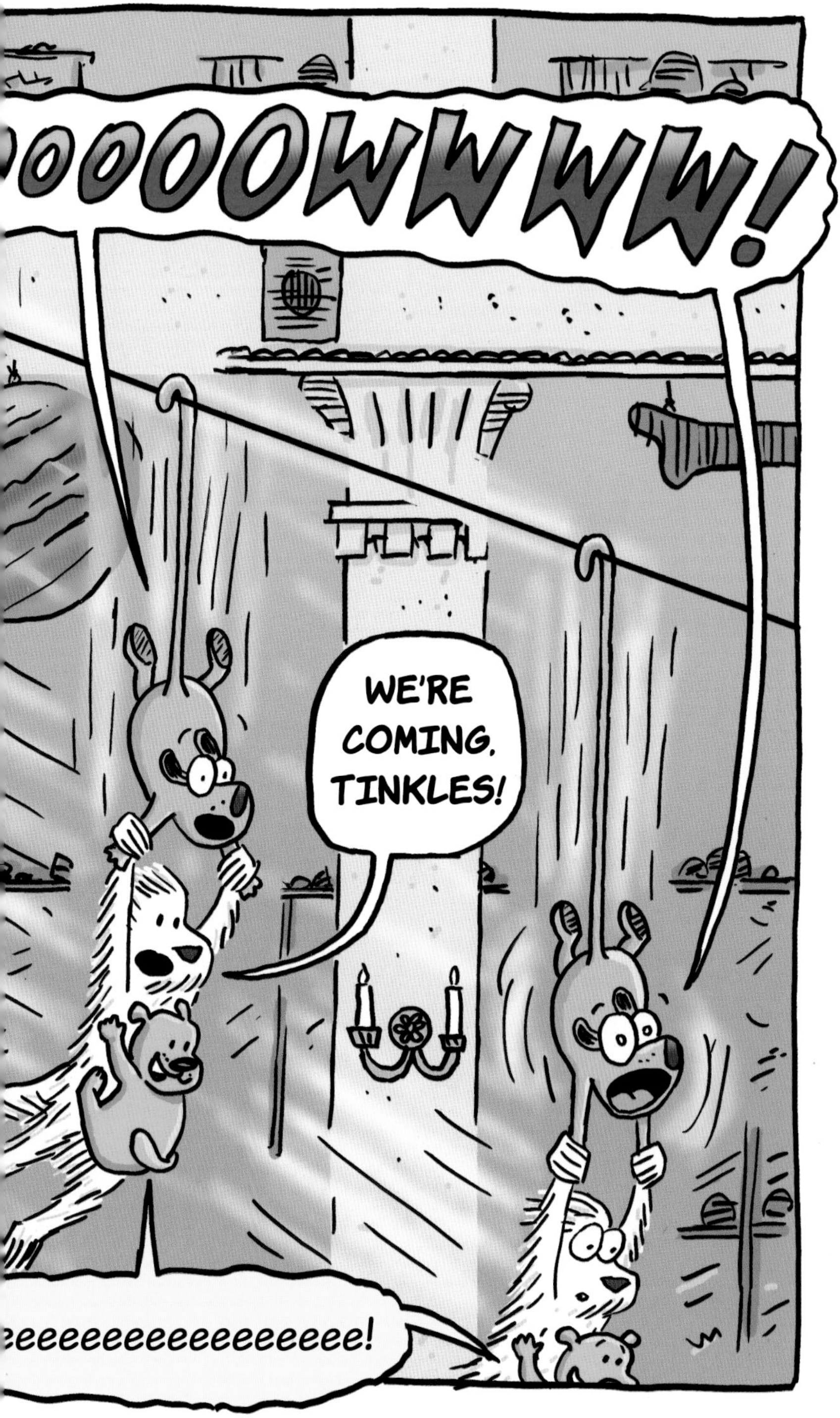

OOOOOOWWWWW!
WE'RE COMING, TINKLES!
eeeeeeeeeeeeeeeeeee!

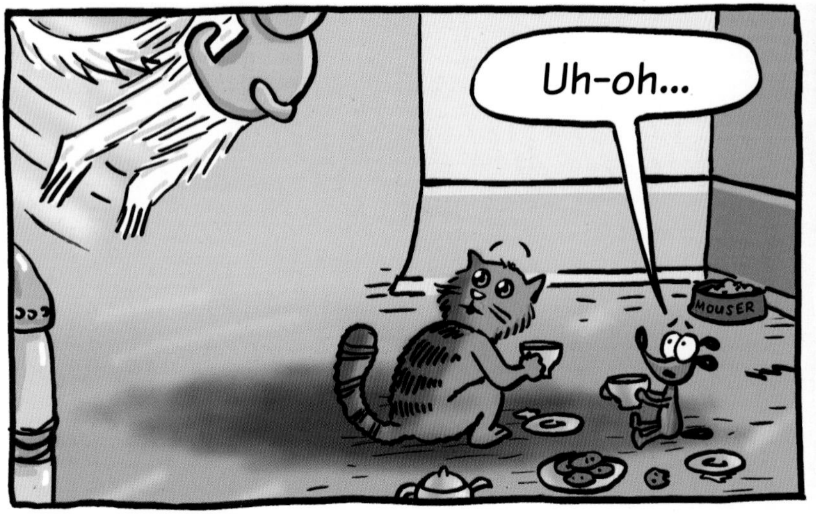
Uh-oh...
MOUSER

The fearless crew swung into battle in a desperate attempt to free Tinkles from the evil Cat-of-Nine-Tails. This could be the end for the Scurvy Dogs.

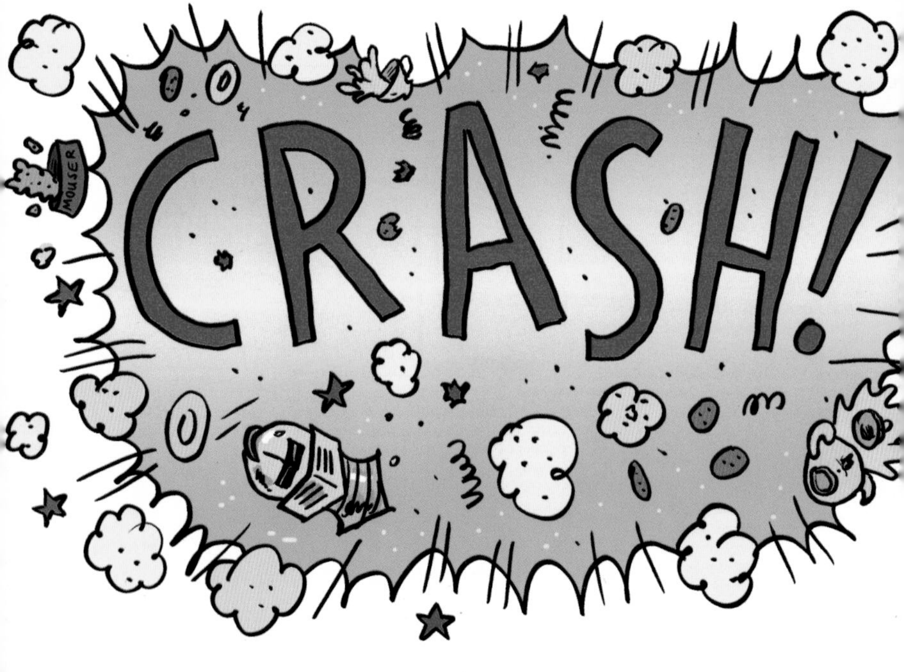
CRASH!
MOUSER

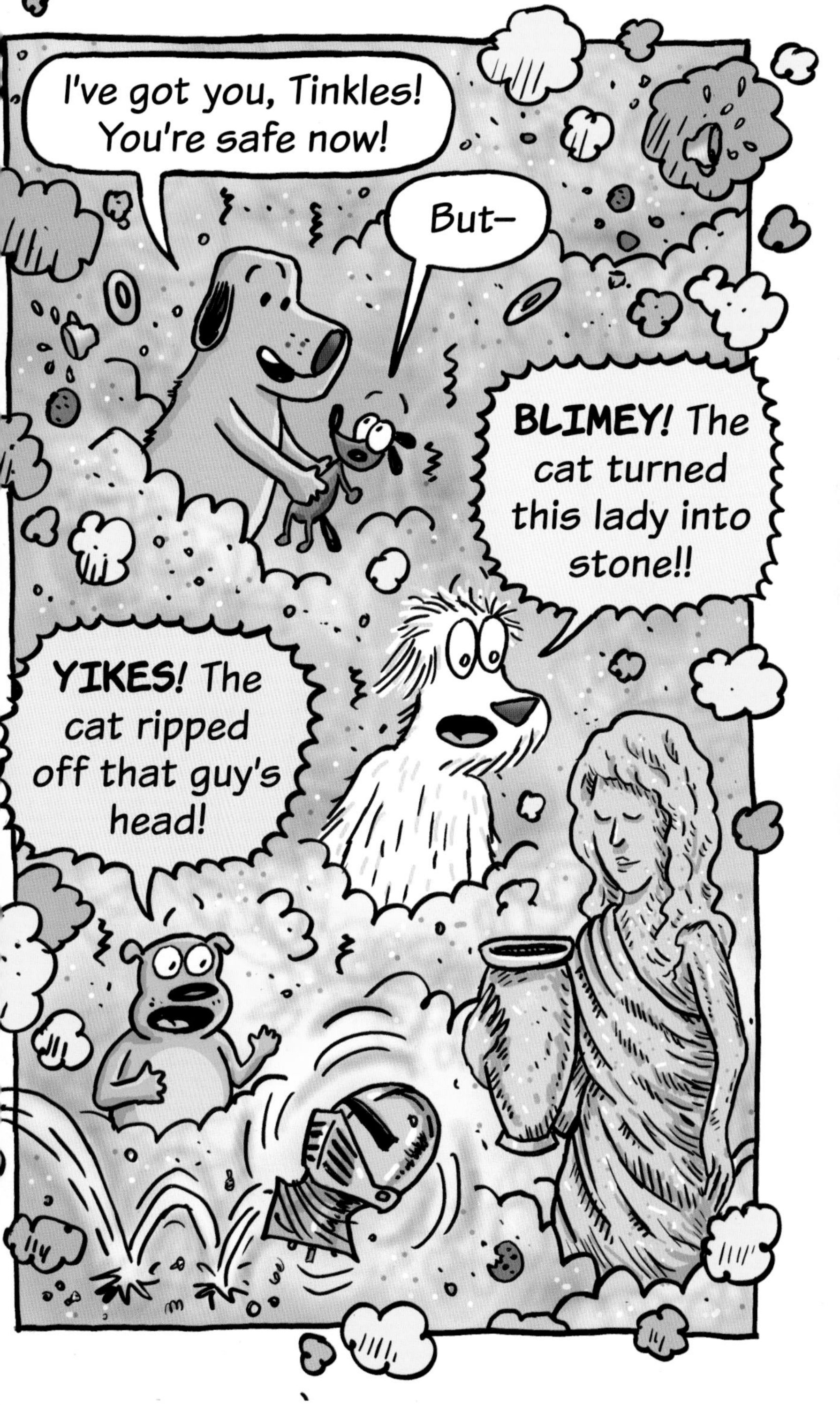

I've got you, Tinkles! You're safe now!
But–
BLIMEY! The cat turned this lady into stone!!
YIKES! The cat ripped off that guy's head!

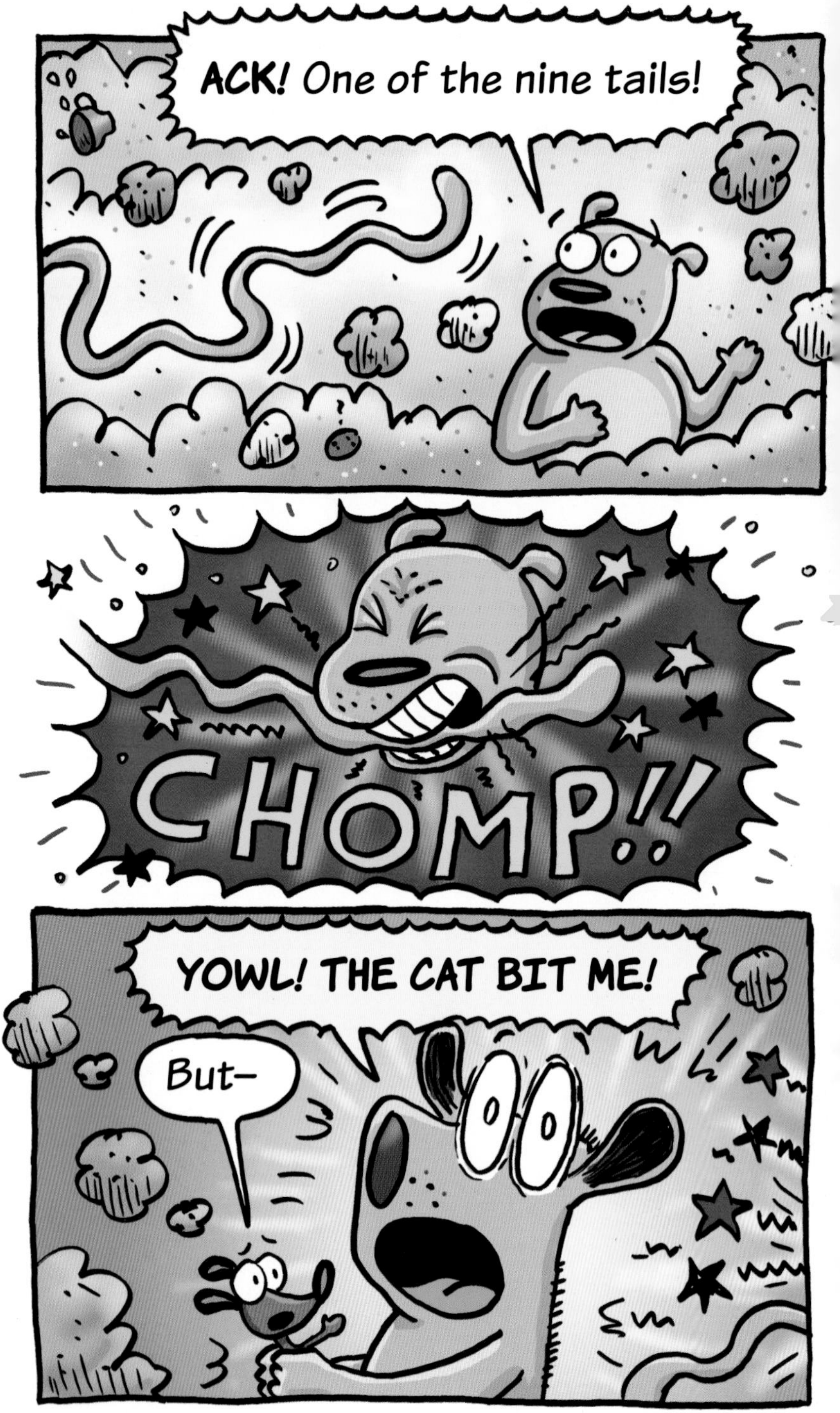
ACK! One of the nine tails!
CHOMP!!
YOWL! THE CAT BIT ME!
But–

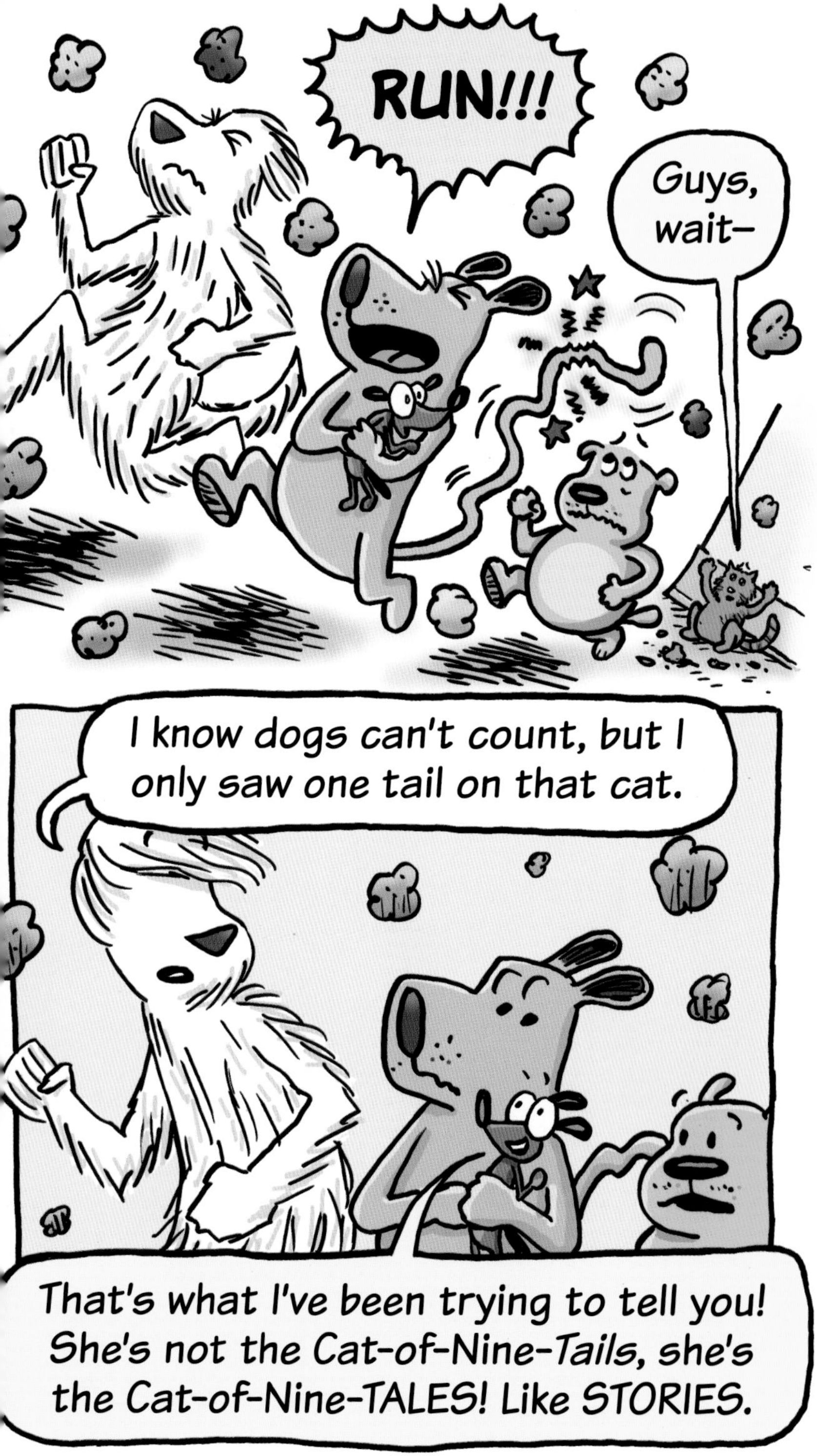
RUN!!!
Guys, wait–
I know dogs can't count, but I only saw one tail on that cat.
That's what I've been trying to tell you! She's not the Cat-of-Nine-*Tails*, she's the Cat-of-Nine-TALES! Like STORIES.

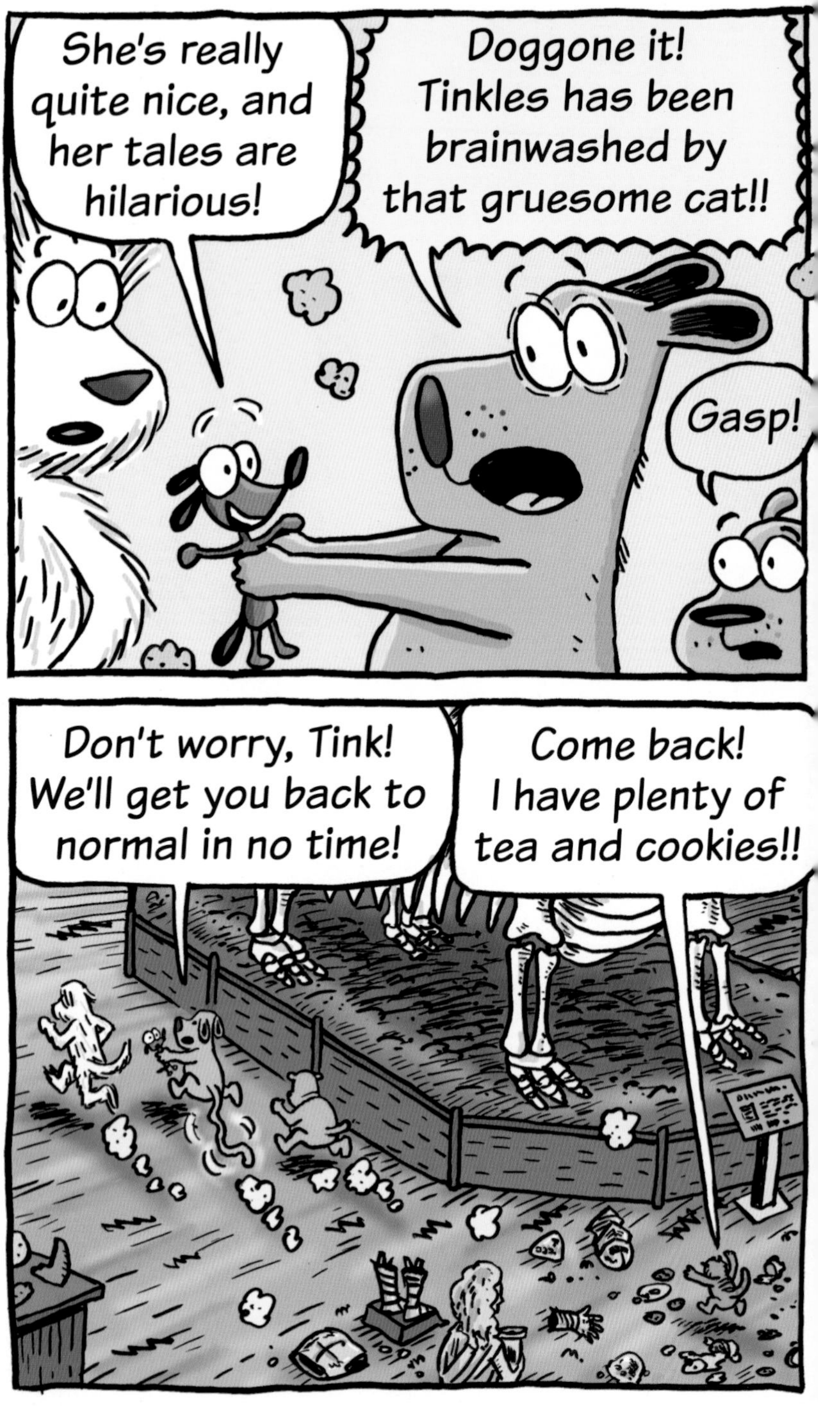
She's really quite nice, and her tales are hilarious!
Doggone it! Tinkles has been brainwashed by that gruesome cat!!
Gasp!
Don't worry, Tink! We'll get you back to normal in no time!
Come back! I have plenty of tea and cookies!!

Chapter Eight

The vile Cat-of-Nine-Tails chased after the crew. It was probably trying to brainwash them all like it did poor confused Tinkles!

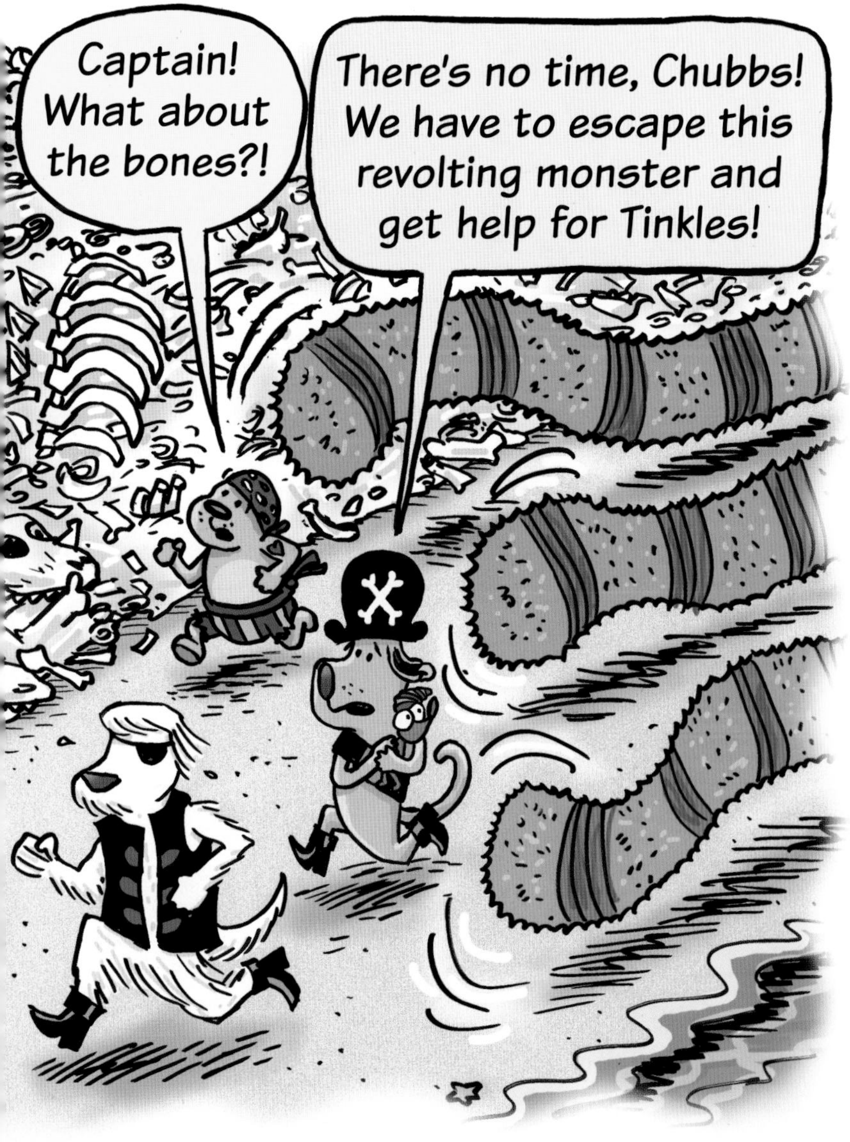
Captain! What about the bones?!
There's no time, Chubbs! We have to escape this revolting monster and get help for Tinkles!

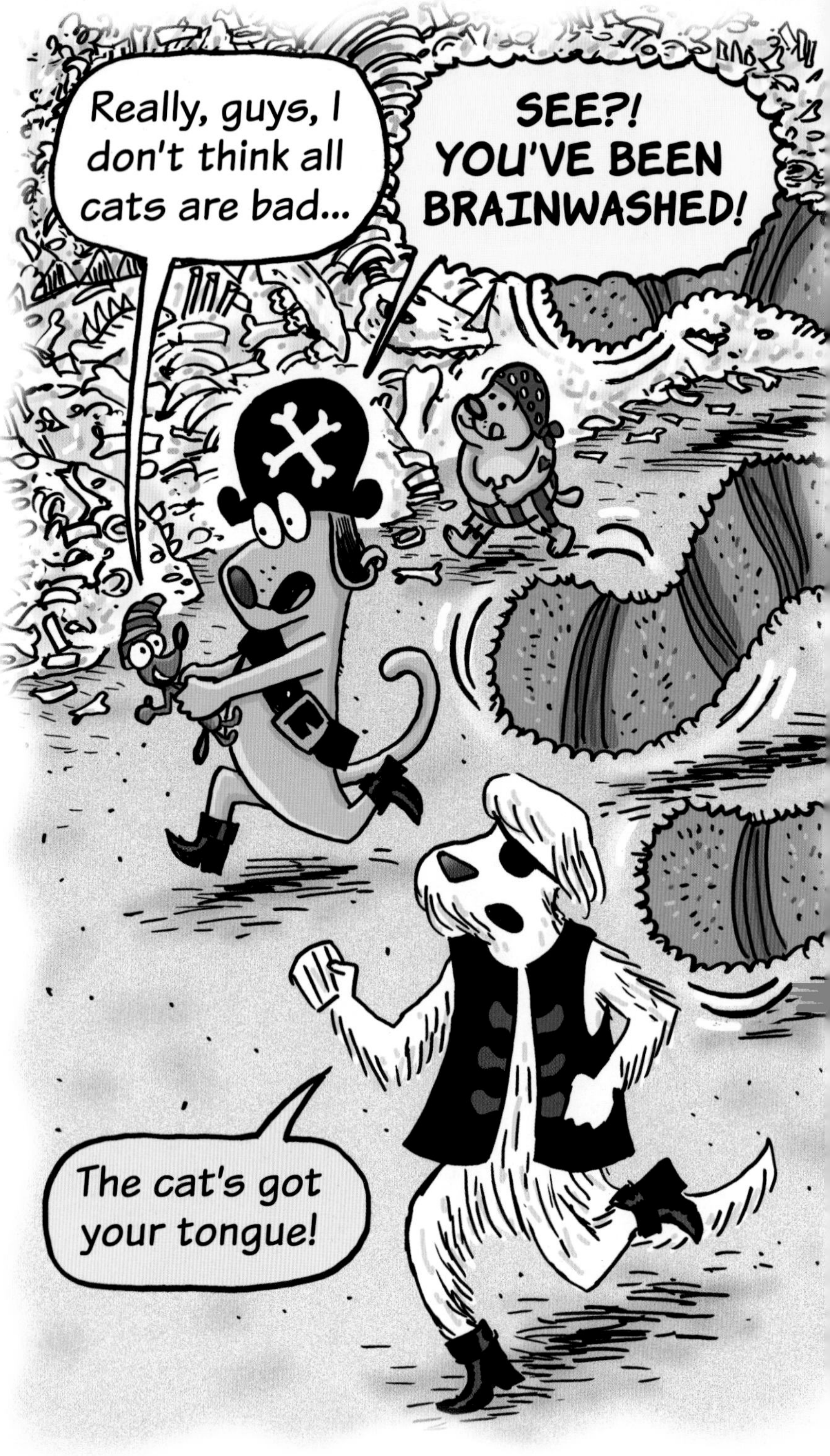
Really, guys, I don't think all cats are bad...
SEE?! YOU'VE BEEN BRAINWASHED!
The cat's got your tongue!

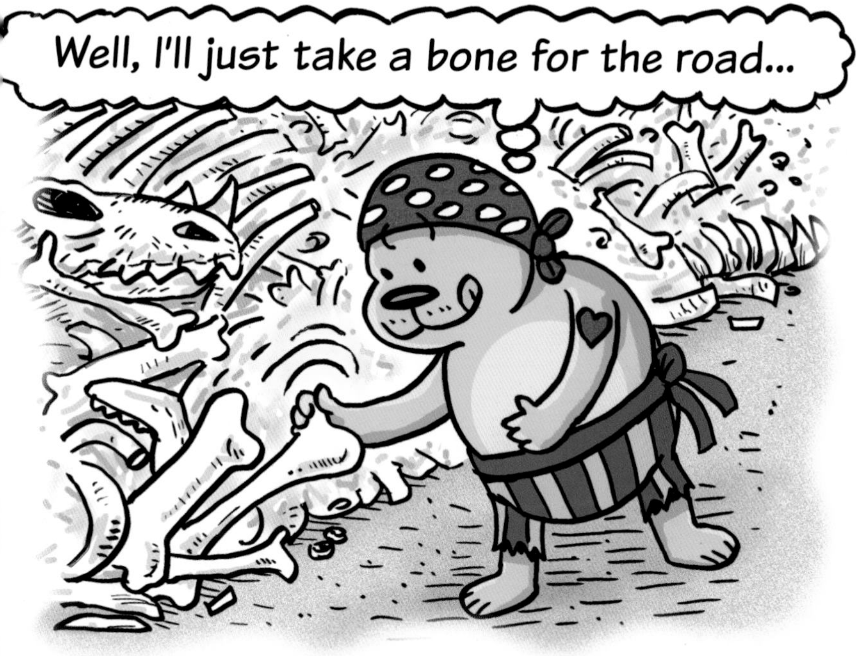
Well, I'll just take a bone for the road...

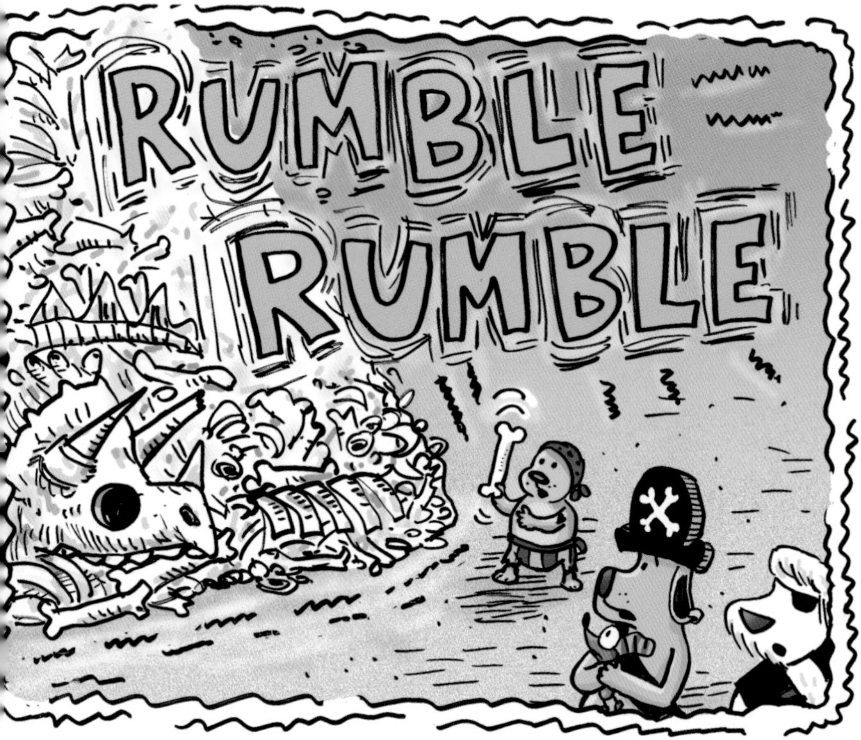
RUMBLE
RUMBLE

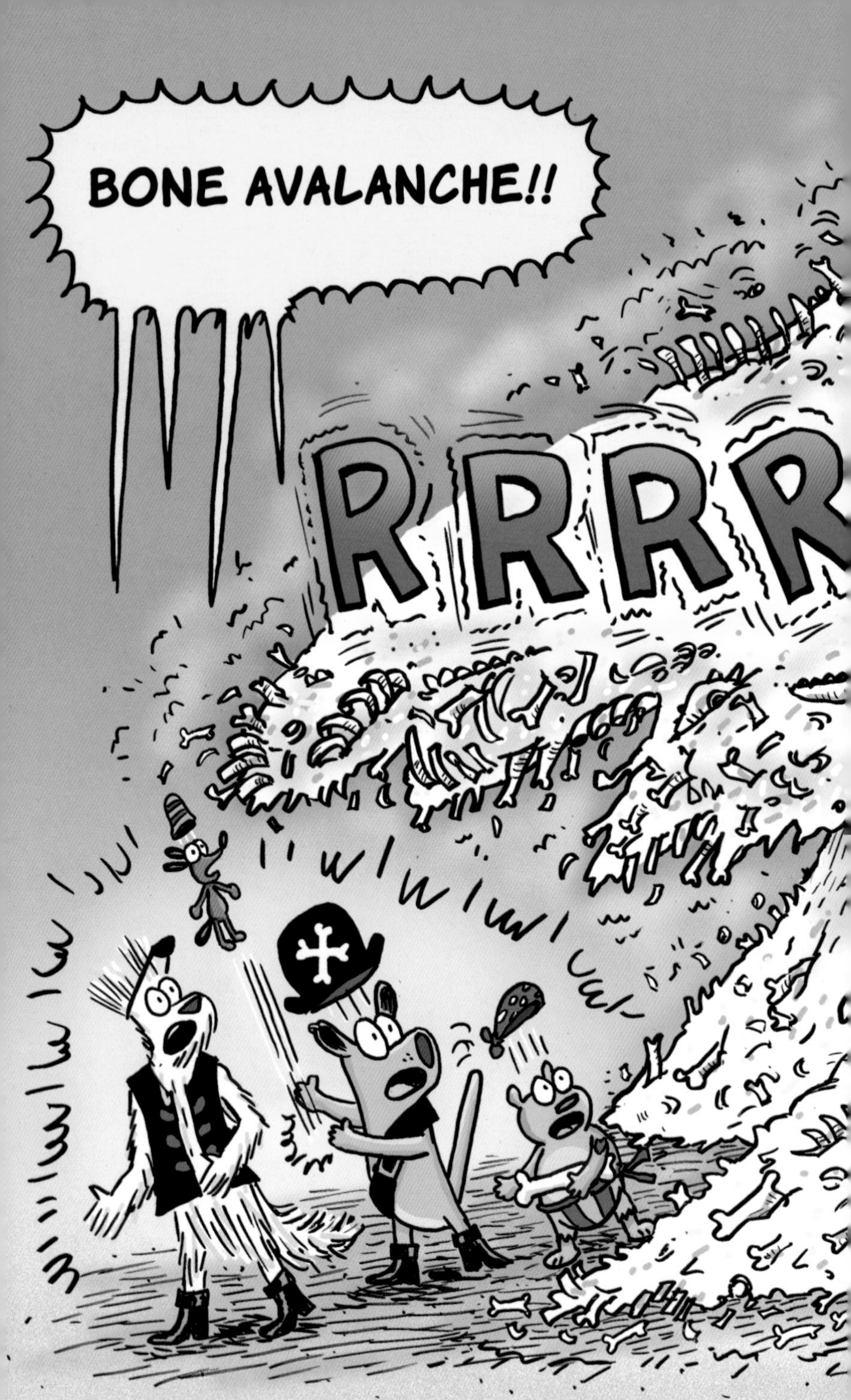
BONE AVALANCHE!!
RRRR

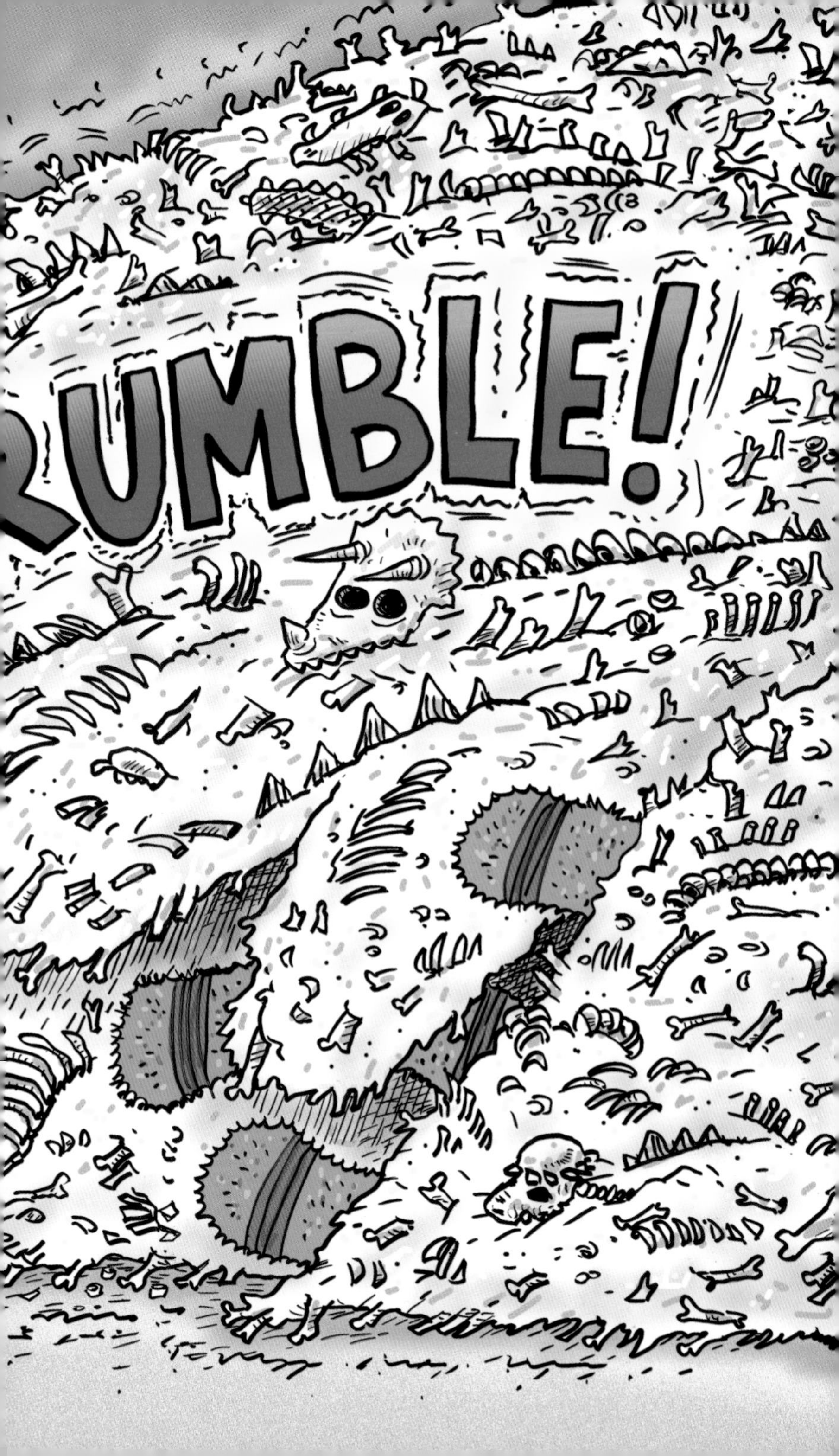
RUMBLE!

Dinosaur bones crashed behind the dogs in a deafening roar!

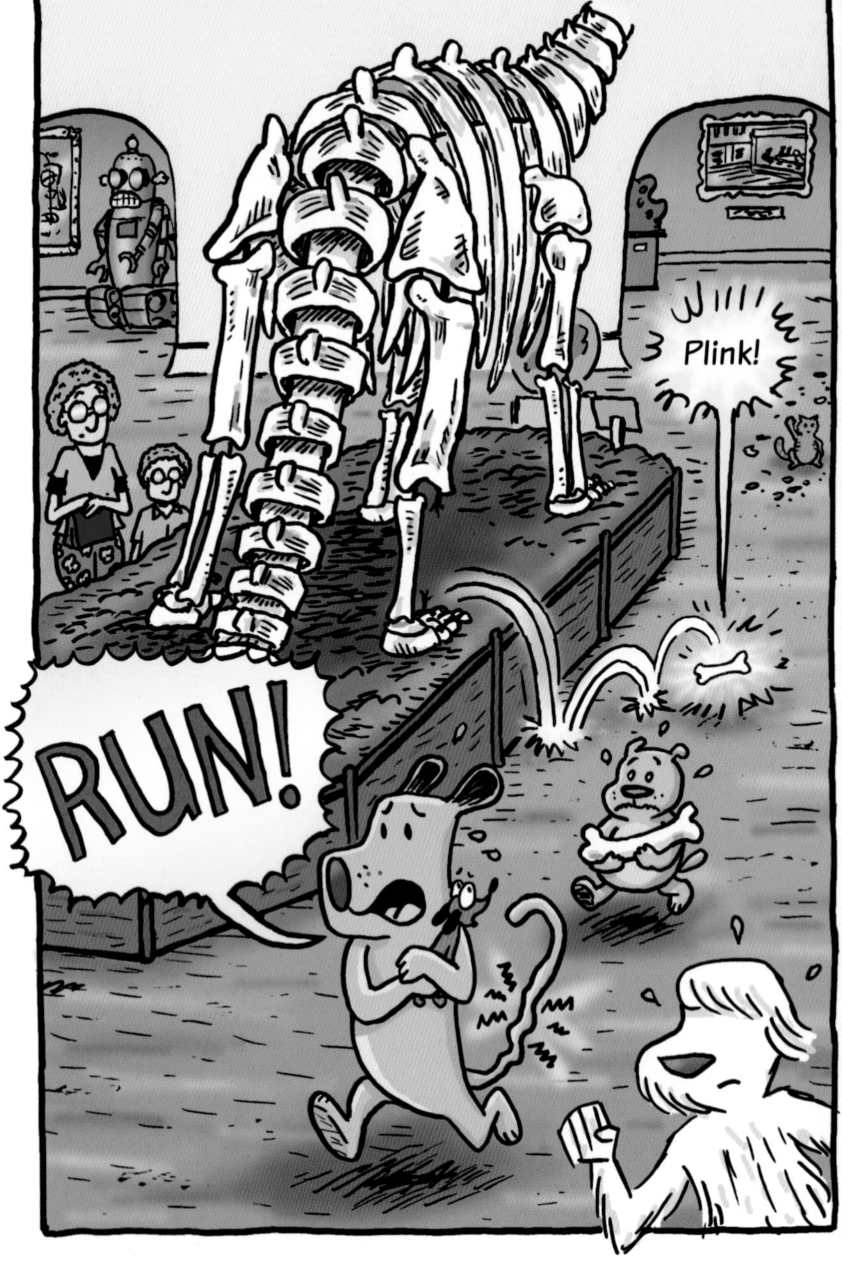
Plink!
RUN!

The good news is that the bone avalanche buried the Cat-of-Nine-Tails. The bad news is that the Scurvy Dogs were next!

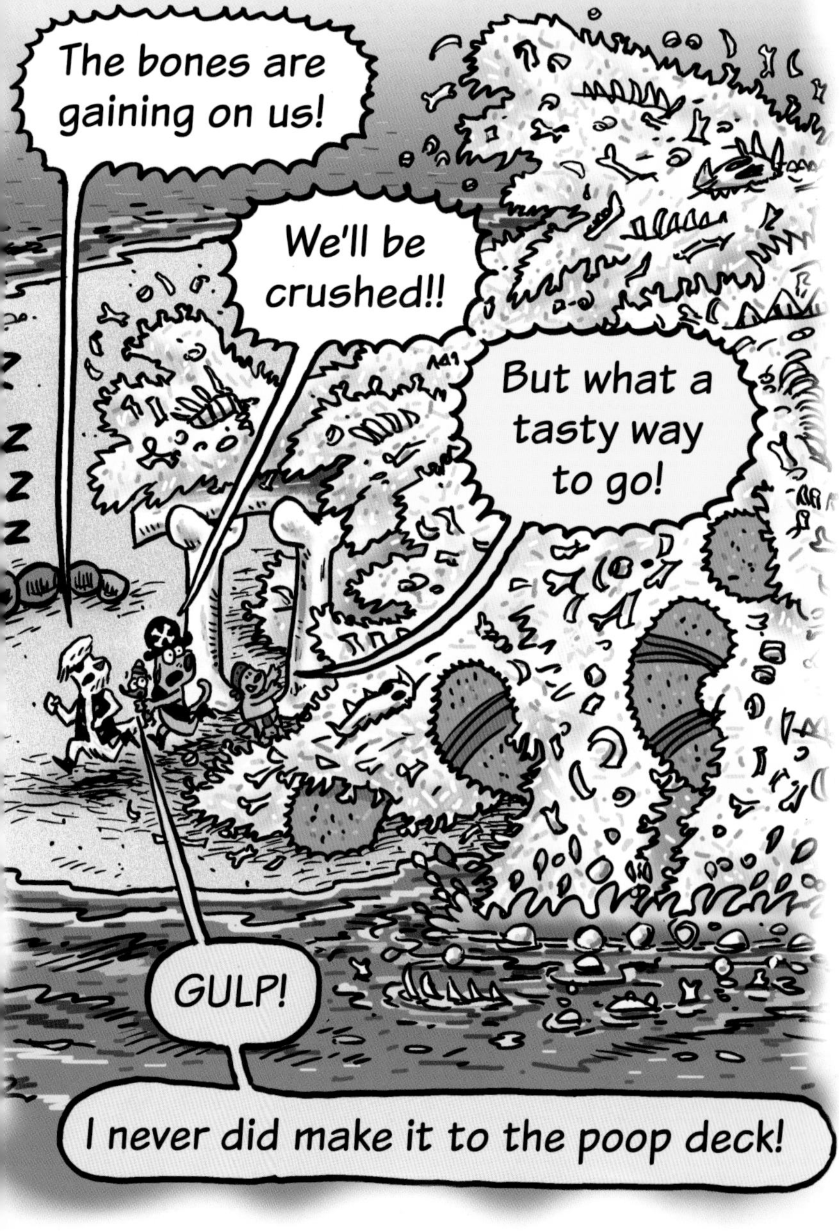
The bones are gaining on us!
We'll be crushed!!
But what a tasty way to go!
ZZZ
GULP!
I never did make it to the poop deck!

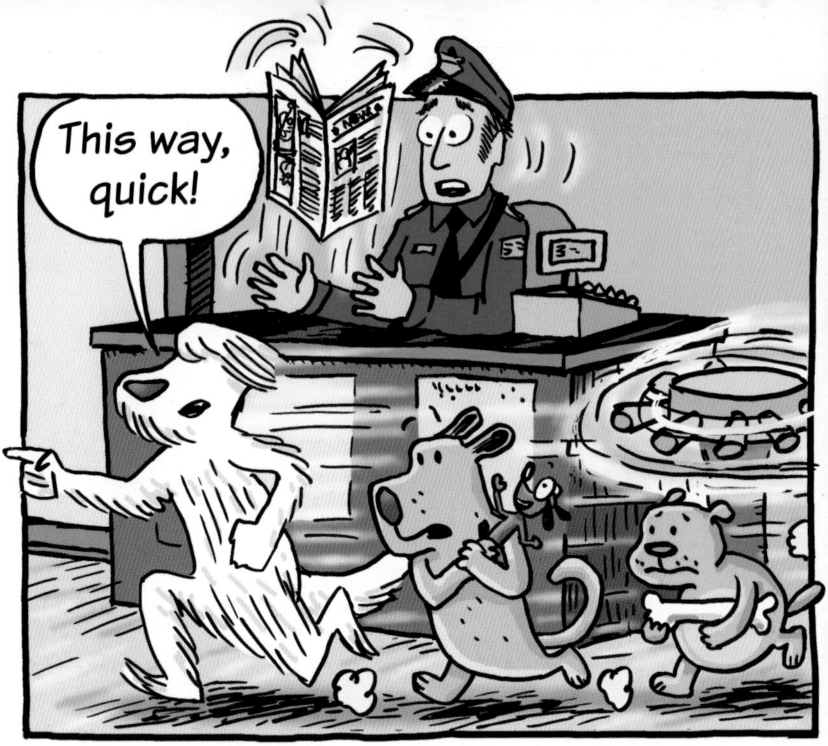
This way, quick!

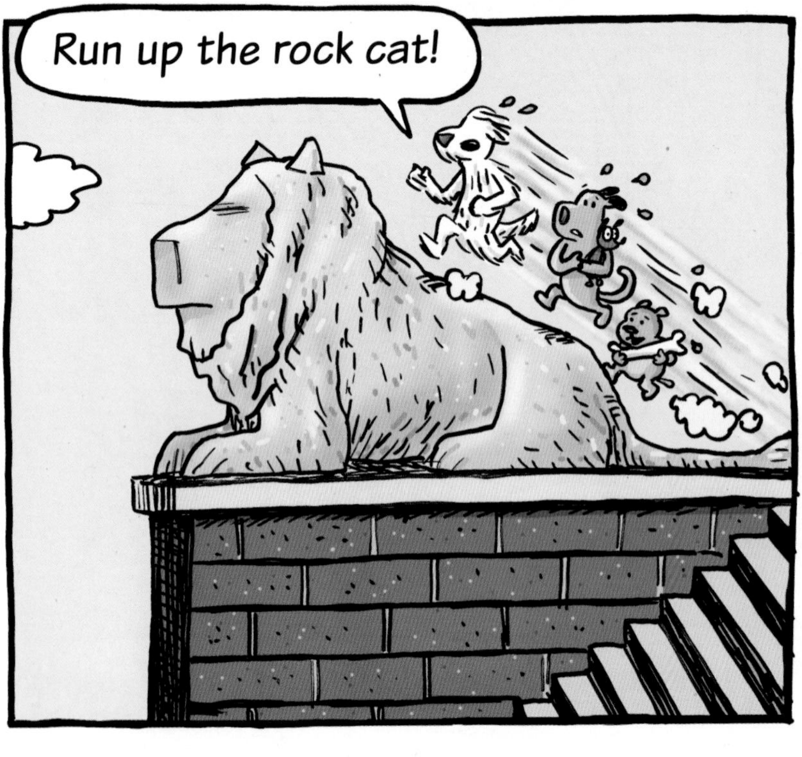
Run up the rock cat!

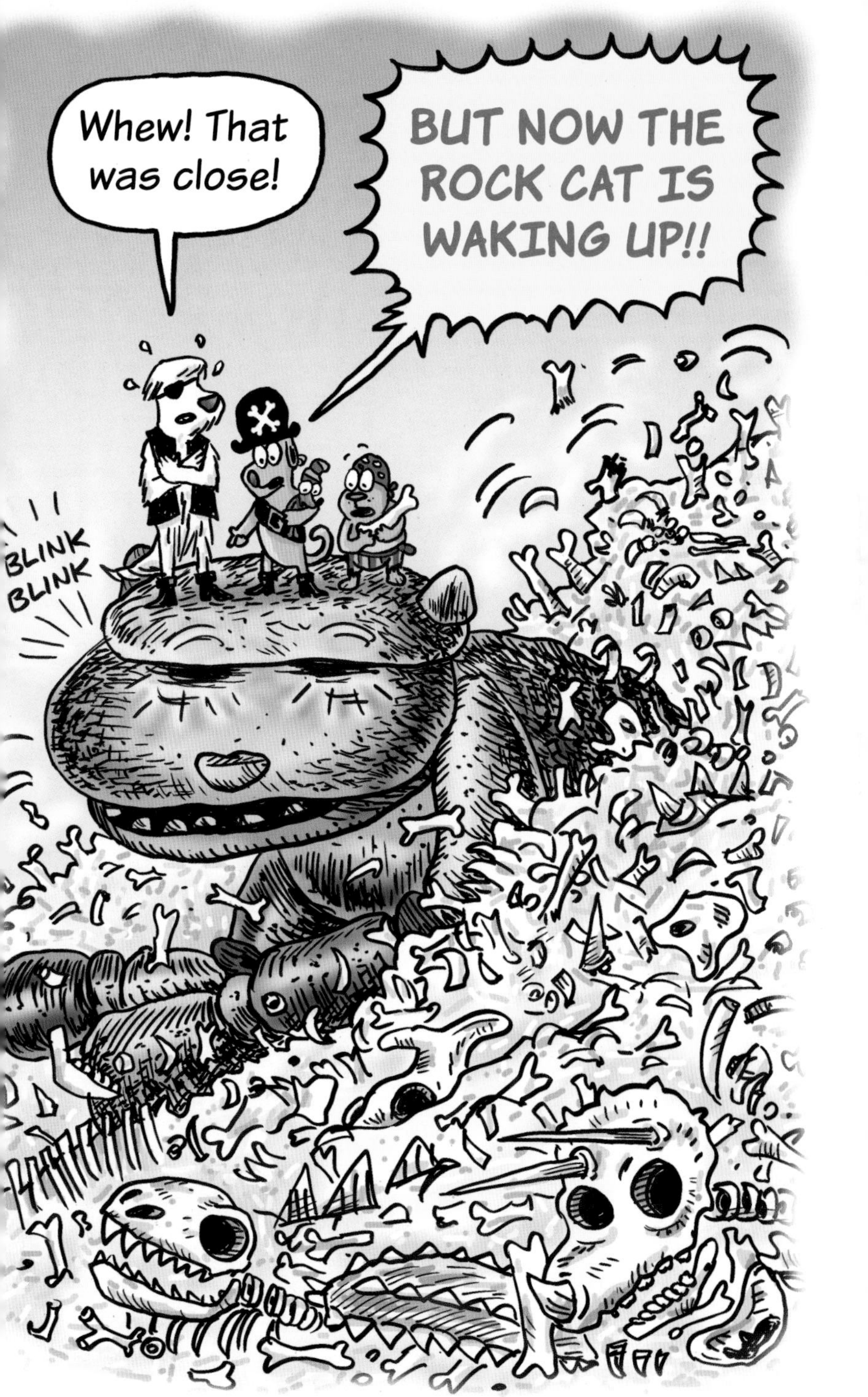
Whew! That was close!
BUT NOW THE ROCK CAT IS WAKING UP!!
BLINK
BLINK

Everyone knows that cats HATE to be disturbed when they're napping!

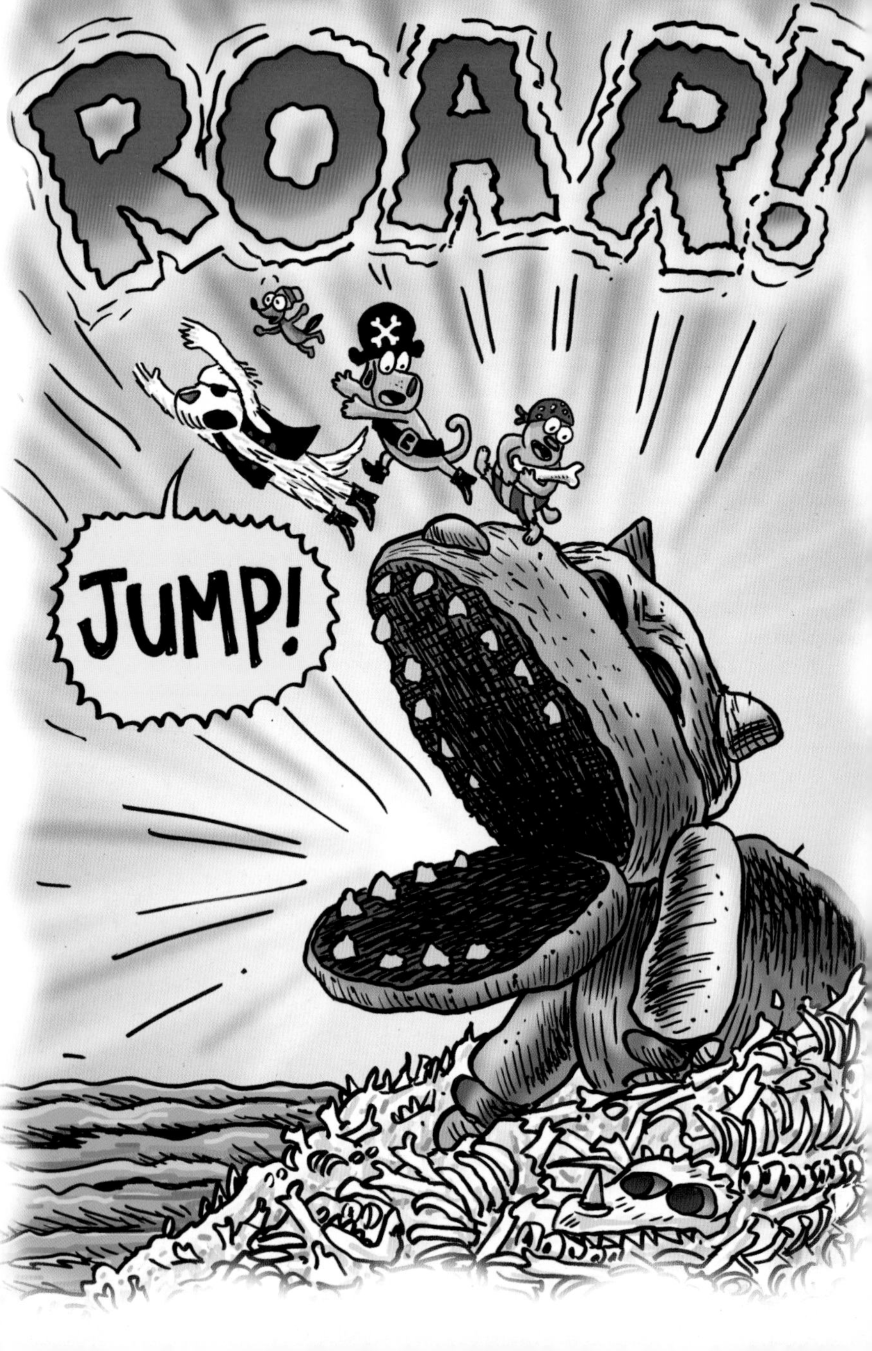

ROAR!
JUMP!

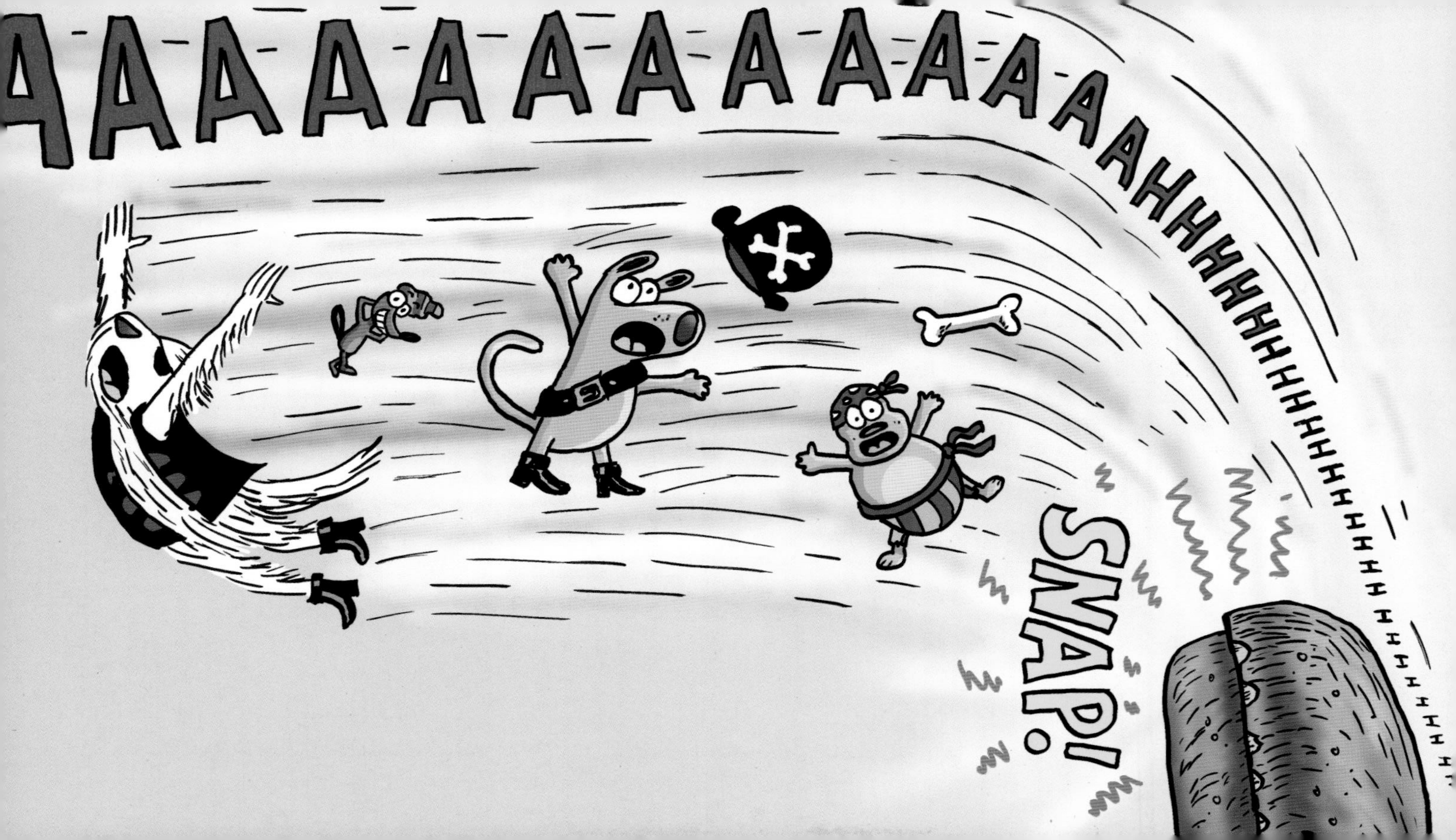
AAAAAAAAAAAAAHHHHHHHHHHHHHHHHHHHHHHHHHHHHH
SNAP!

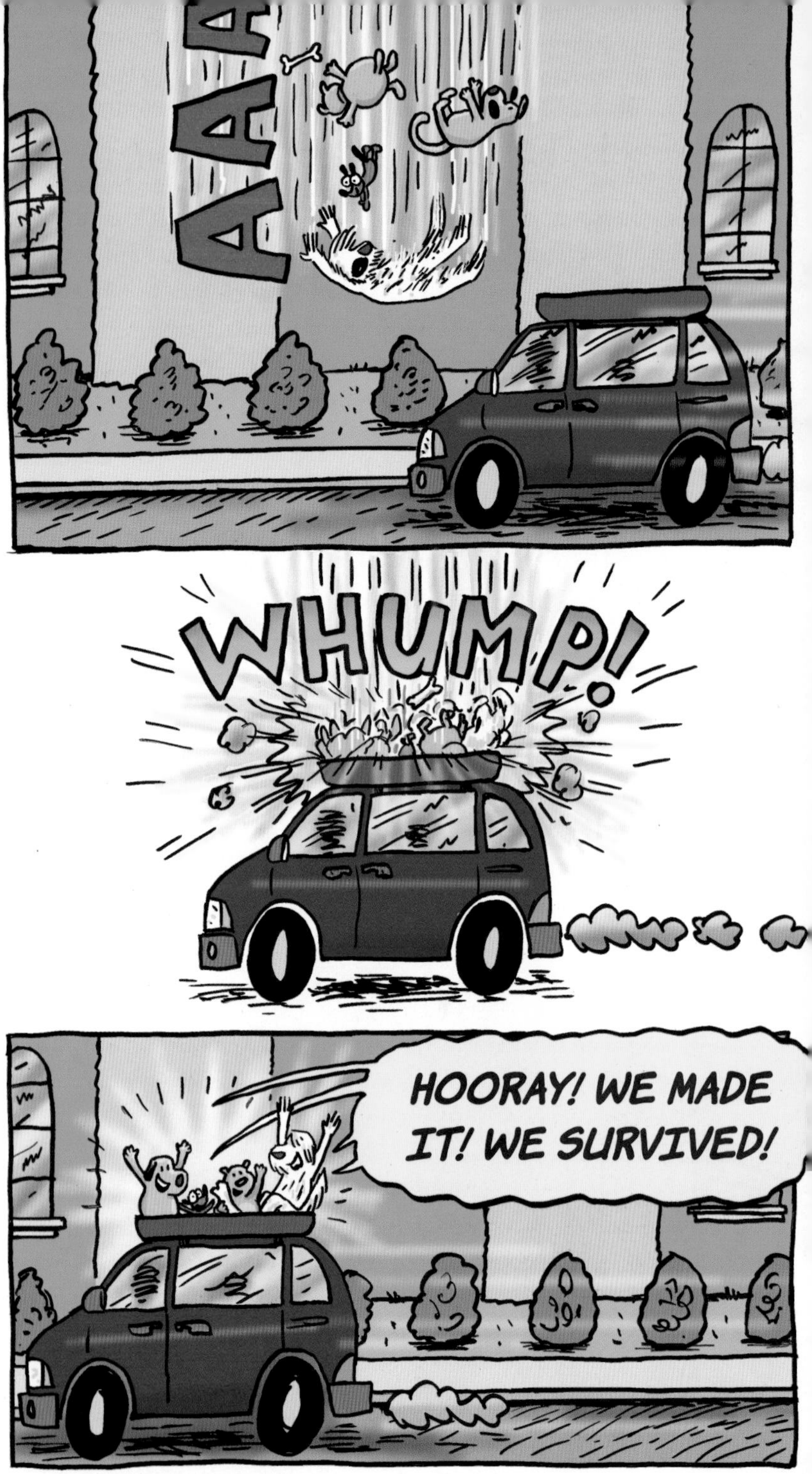
AAA
WHUMP!
HOORAY! WE MADE IT! WE SURVIVED!

Our heroes landed safely back aboard their ship as the rock cats roared in frustration. And since the Dinosaur Boneyard was now a dusty ruin, the Scurvy Dogs set sail for home.

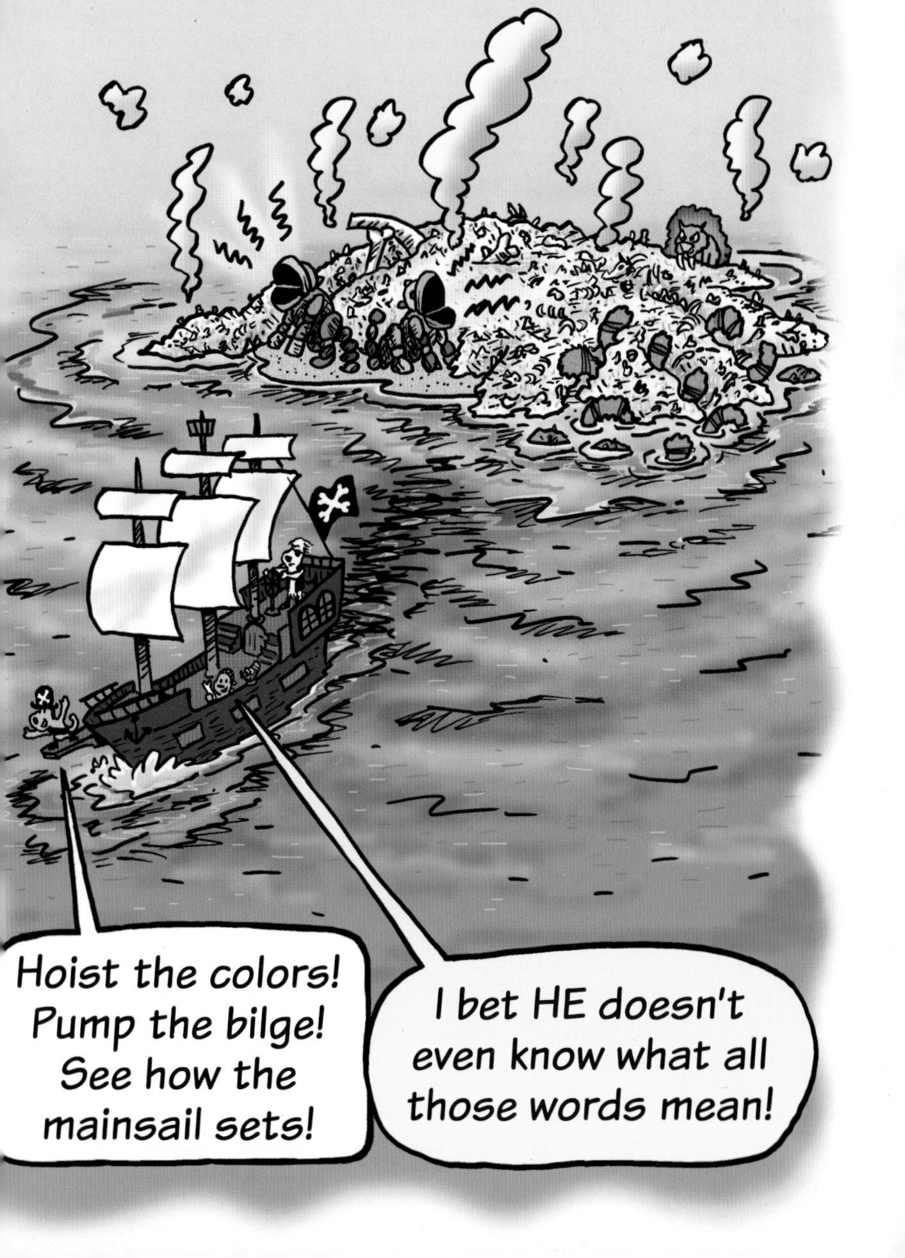

Hoist the colors! Pump the bilge! See how the mainsail sets!
I bet HE doesn't even know what all those words mean!

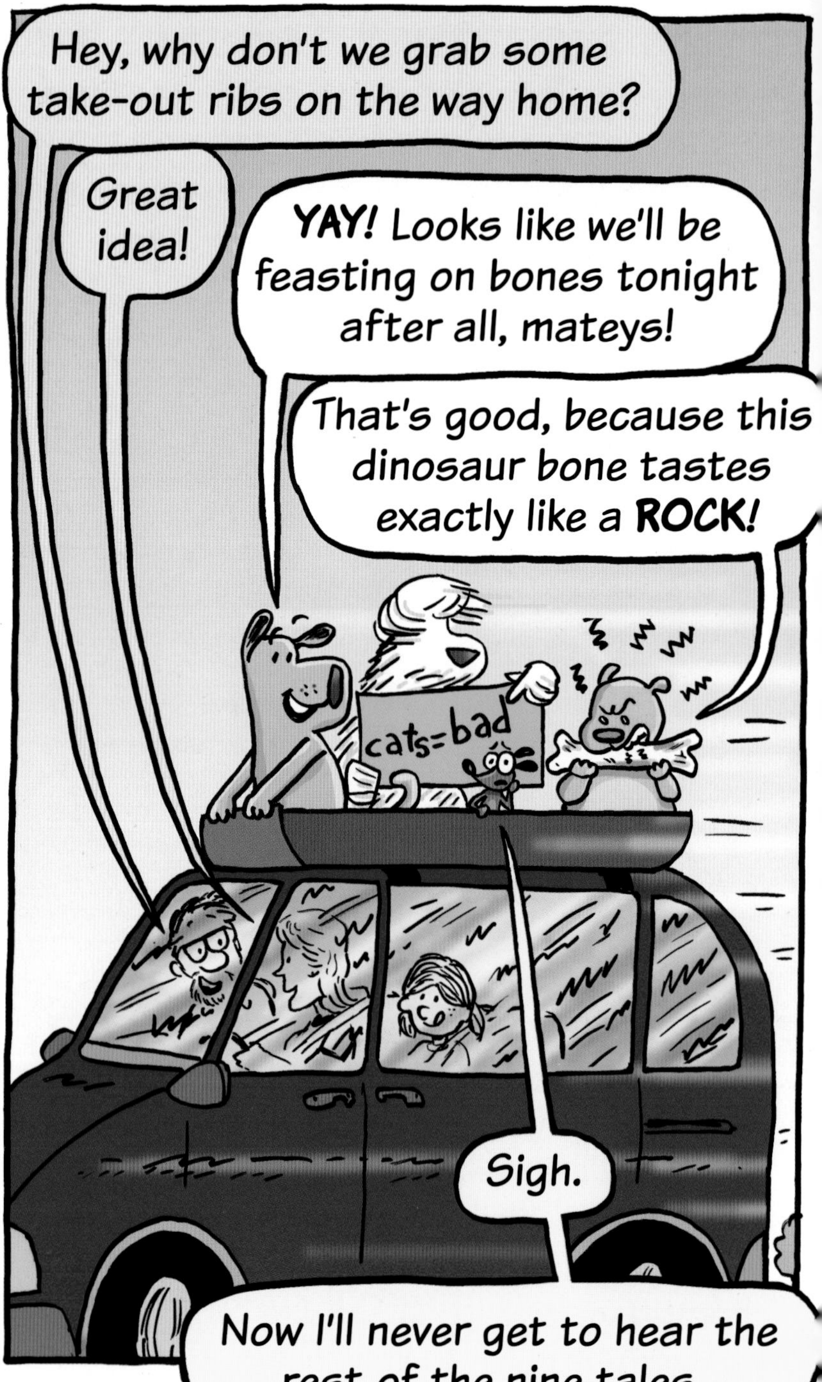
Hey, why don't we grab some take-out ribs on the way home?
Great idea!
YAY! Looks like we'll be feasting on bones tonight after all, mateys!
That's good, because this dinosaur bone tastes exactly like a ROCK!
cats=bad
Sigh.
Now I'll never get to hear the rest of the nine tales.

About the author

Kevin Frank is an award-winning author and
illustrator. Originally from Illinois, he now calls
a small town in Canada home. He steals his best
material from his wife and three children.
Visit him at www.kevinfrank.net